Blueberry Boys

VANESSA NORTH

RIPTIDE
PUBLISHING

Riptide Publishing
PO Box 6652
Hillsborough, NJ 08844
www.riptidepublishing.com

Blueberry Boys
Copyright © 2015 by Vanessa North

Cover art: L.C. Chase, lcchase.com/design.htm
Editor: Carole-ann Galloway
Layout: L.C. Chase, lcchase.com/design.htm

ISBN: 978-1-62649-342-1

First edition
November, 2015

Also available in ebook:
ISBN: 978-1-62649-341-4

Blueberry
Boys

VANESSA
NORTH

RIPTIDE
PUBLISHING

To Mishy Jo

Table
of Contents

Chapter One

Blueberries. Row upon row, acre upon acre. Connor's arms ached with the memory of his first summer job. The dew glinting off the grass and leaves set his heart thumping thickly in his chest. Six said it was nostalgia, half dozen said grief. He lifted his camera from where it hung heavy around his neck and snapped a few photos. It was early yet; the golden hour hadn't arrived, so there wouldn't be any magic in the images. But he hadn't come out here to make magic. He'd come to make a eulogy.

How many times could one man say good-bye to the same place?

He heard the diesel engine long before he bothered to turn around. This would be Bruce's—no, Scott and Connor's—tenant, probably wondering what Connor was doing here. Sure enough, the dually rumbled to a stop beside him, and a slender man about his own age stepped down from the cab. Brown hair and eyes, a hint of crow's feet around the latter, unremarkable and yet appealing. Beautiful in that way strangers were, before you learned they hated cats or liked the wrong kind of country music.

"This is pr-private property. You c-can't shoot pictures here." The tenant's voice was quiet, but with a firm set to his chin, he clearly meant business.

"It's okay." Connor tried to find a smile to offer him, but all he had was his name. "I'm Connor Graham."

The man's smile faded, and he ducked his head, swiping his Red Sox hat down and into his palms. "Man. I'm s-sorry. About your uncle."

"Thank you. You're the tenant, right? I'm sorry, I don't know your name." *I hold his future in my hands; I should know his name.*

"Jed J-Jones."

Hell of a name for a man with a stutter.

Jed extended his hand slowly, like an afterthought. Connor reached to grasp it and ended up holding the hat. Jed flushed, grabbed it back, and placed it on his head with an exasperated *huff.* Then he took Connor's hand in his, shaking firmly.

Jed's hands were thin like the rest of him, fingernails stained purple around the edges. Connor didn't know whether that spoke to his work ethic or his grooming habits, but found these farmer's hands striking. He let go and lifted his camera.

"May I?"

"It's your farm." No bitterness there, just acquiescence.

"No, I mean, may I take your portrait?"

Jed's face shuttered. "W-what for?"

"Because the first hour after sunrise, the world turns gold and gorgeous. Any minute now, the light is going to catch every bush here on fire—it's going to be amazing. You're here, you're part of it, and I'd like you to be in the photograph."

"Out here with b-burning bushes?" Jed raised a soft brown eyebrow and smiled.

"Please?"

"I guess." He shrugged, then took off his baseball cap again. His hair was flattened close to his head, but puffed out a little around his ears. *Hat head.* Not something Connor was used to seeing in the city among the darlings of the male model set. And yet Jed lifted his chin with a model's instincts, and the line of his jaw, the jut of his cheekbones were thrown into prominence. *Beautiful.*

"Here." Connor pointed to the end of a row of bushes. "Stand just to the right of this one." He stepped back and waited for the light. Jed studied Connor for a long moment—bemused or annoyed, Connor couldn't tell—then turned his face to the east and watched in silence.

Jed was painted in gold and rose as the sun crept above the horizon. All around him, the sunlight caught on dew, limning the branches and leaves and casting a halo around Jed's hair. It was almost enough to make Connor believe in angels. *But not quite.*

The clicks of Connor's shutter sounded rapid-fire, loud in the morning stillness. Sure, he'd come out here to take photos of the farm, but this, this was so much better. This was the kind of portrait that won awards—a modern farmer, his baseball cap under his arm as he greeted the dawn. It felt intimate, sacred even. Connor wasn't a lifestyle photographer, nor a documentarian. A photograph like this, of a man in his element, seemed surreal to someone who plied his trade in the carefully crafted falsehoods of fashion photography.

Jed turned his face back to Connor, smiled, and said, soft as can be, "Ch-cheese."

Connor snapped a last shot and then lowered the camera. "Thanks."

Jed ducked his head and nodded.

"I'll let you go back to work." Connor gestured to the truck. "I'll take a few more photos of the farm, if that's okay."

"It's y-your farm." Jed repeated with a shrug. "I just work it."

Connor nodded, awkward in the face of Jed's acceptance of his place here. A place Connor didn't feel a claim to, and didn't want to. "Okay, thanks."

Placing his hat on his head, Jed tipped it gently in Connor's direction and climbed back into his truck. Connor watched him drive away, ignoring the temptation to photograph the tracks he left in the mud like so much graffiti. *Jed was here.* He wasn't what Connor had expected when Marty Sullivan told him there was a tenant living in the main house and working the land.

The farmers he'd known as a child had been men like his uncle— big, brawny, and well used to a day's work. Jed Jones was built like he'd fall over in a strong wind, with a body more in common with the lithe young things Connor photographed than with the rednecks who'd had no patience for Bruce Graham's chubby sissy-boy nephew.

"Ch-cheese."

Models didn't say "Cheese."

Connor took more photos, following the light across the landscape—still golden and glorious—but the feeling of capturing something special had ridden away with Jed Jones and his dually.

Not twenty minutes later, a truck rolled up and gangly high school kids with their braces and their awkward flirtations piled out and set to work removing berries from the bushes. The wet *thunk* of berries dropping into the buckets they wore around their necks made

Connor smile as he remembered working next to his friend Kyle Bauer, trying not to stare at his muscular legs, or to laugh harder at his jokes than anyone else did. That summer, Connor had still thought he had secrets.

"Hey Connor, check this out!" Kyle held out a blueberry the size of a half-dollar. "You ever seen one this big?"

Connor shook his head, wiping sweat from his eyes, and dumped the contents of his bucket in the carrier at his feet. Purple pints today. An expensive variety. Bruce didn't usually trust the teens with these.

"Here, you have it, if I eat any more blueberries, I'm gonna be sick."

And then Kyle's hand was at Connor's mouth, stifling a gasp of shock by slipping the berry between open lips. The dry brush of Kyle's thumb whispered across Connor's lower lip and the sweetness of the berry broke across his tongue.

Connor shuddered, remembering the innocent touch and Kyle's awkward smile, followed by a shrug. They'd both had boners tenting their shorts, though neither had said anything. What'd ever happened to Kyle Bauer?

Several rows down, another truck dropped a crew of adult workers who spoke a language Connor didn't recognize, laughing easily with each other. This crew was mostly women, but with a few men too, and they worked with an efficiency the kids lacked. They would harvest twice as many berries as the kids, but they wouldn't enjoy themselves half as much. Once they spotted Connor, there was a grimness to the way they moved, and they gave him curious glances, eyeing his camera warily. *Time to go.*

Lights shone inside the farm offices when he returned to where he'd parked his rental car, so Connor headed up the familiar steps to the little trailer where Bruce used to hand out paychecks. He knocked, which felt weird because he owned it, but appropriate because he was a stranger to whoever worked inside. He'd just get an email address to send the portrait to, and then he'd be on his way.

"Come in!"

Stepping into the trailer was like stepping back in time. The same ugly desk and chairs, the same card table—though a new microwave. The same stifling lack of air conditioning. On the floor next to the desk, a toddler in a diaper made engine noises as he pushed his blocks around on ancient stained carpet. The kid had the same light-brown hair as Jed Jones, and he flashed Connor a drooly smile.

"Can I help you?" The woman behind the desk smiled expectantly. She was familiar in a way that made Connor think she was from around here but not Blandford. He racked his brain for a name, finally gave up, and introduced himself.

"I'm Connor Graham."

Her face fell, and she extended her hand. "Of course, I should have known. Hannah Jones—you probably don't remember me from school, I was a freshman when you were a junior—my maiden name was Bradshaw. I'm so sorry for your loss."

"Hannah Bradshaw," he repeated, suddenly placing her. "You played Éponine when the high school did *Les Mis*. Better than at least one I've seen on Broadway." Easy and completely untrue flattery, but it made her blush and smile, so he couldn't regret the lie.

"You're kind to say so."

The door opened behind him and Jed walked in, pausing when he saw Connor. He pulled off his hat and gave a gruff nod, which Connor returned.

Jed glanced at the child on the floor and sort of grimaced, then said, "Hannah, we got sh-shoestring in the Rancocas. Can you call M-Mike and get him out here to help me? S-same pay."

"You got it." She picked up the phone on the desk and started dialing.

Jed turned to Connor. "You get all the p-pictures you need?"

Connor nodded. "I was just leaving. That thing, the shoestring thing . . . is it serious?"

"Hopefully it's j-just the one plant. Won't impact the value of your land."

"But your crop?"

"Is n-n-none of your business."

Gone was the soft-smiling man Connor had met in the field at dawn. In his place was another hard-faced farmer, worried about pests and disease and scowling at children. God, they were all alike, weren't they?

"I wasn't asking because I was worried about money. I was worried for you. Forget it."

Jed's face softened. "W-we'll be fine."

"Okay, then. I'm going to go. Do you have an email address? I can send you the photos I took."

He glanced at his shoes. "We're on F-Facebook. The f-farm. You can send them there."

"I'll look you up." Connor offered his tenant—because that's who Jed was, not a model to be photographed, but the man renting Connor's land—a hesitant smile, then backed his way out of the trailer.

Jed watched out the window as his new landlord got into a little silver rental car and drove away. He was only halfheartedly listening to his sister-in-law call Mike to ask for help. It had been a long time since Jed had examined the blueberries and seen anything other than profit. Or loss. That it was his new landlord who made him see poetry there—well, he wasn't quite sure what to think about that. Wasn't sure what to think about the way Graham had regarded him either—meeting his eyes and lighting up like he saw poetry in Jed, too. It gave him all kinds of butterflies in his stomach. Damn. He shook his head and glanced over his shoulder, just in time to see Billy trying to climb the card table.

"W-whoa, little buddy. That th-thing is not g-gonna hold your weight." He scooped up the toddler. "You sick again?"

Billy stuck two fingers in his mouth and laid his chubby head on Jed's shoulder. "Thed," he said around his fingers.

"Yeah, B-Billy."

"Mike'll be here shortly, he just needs to finish up a brake job." Hannah came around the coffee table to take Billy. "I'm sorry I had to bring him with me today. Dev can't take the kids if they've had a fever within twenty-four hours, and he had a small one last night. I think it was just teething, but what can you do? I'm sorry I didn't tell you ahead of time."

"J-just took me by surprise."

"So, that's the new landlord." She jutted her chin toward the door. "I went to high school with him. He remembered me in the class play. Isn't that a queer thing to remember?"

"Yep." Jed peered out the window again, even though Connor Graham's car was long gone. He didn't know if Hannah meant queer like weird, or queer like him, but he wasn't about to ask.

"Think they're gonna sell?"

Jed's stomach turned. He hoped not. His current lease had fewer than two years left. Finding a piece of land to farm was hard when you couldn't afford to buy your own. And what else could he do? It wasn't like he could take a job working with people to tide him over until he could afford to buy. If Connor and Scott decided to sell . . . Bitterness swept over him. Some men, men who could talk freely, could call the world their oyster. Any pearls destined for Jed were close to home and to the people who tolerated his stammer.

"I d-don't know."

"Are you going to make an offer if he does?"

"I c-can't. D-don't have e-e-enough. Still paying off my student loans. Maybe—maybe when the l-lease is up."

Hannah placed a soothing hand on his arm. "I didn't mean to upset you, Jedidiah. I just wondered."

"I'll be in the Rancocas. Send M-Mike out."

Four. Four infected plants identified by the time Mike arrived. They could be removed and burned, but if aphids were spreading the disease, who knew how many plants had been compromised already? Jed grimaced and moved to the next bush.

"Here's another one," Mike called from the end of the row as he tied a strip of bright tape around a limb. "What are you going to do?"

"I don't f-fucking know," Jed muttered. "R-reconsider organic certification?"

Mike scowled. "Why you even bother—"

"I b-bother because it's my j-job," Jed snapped, moving to the next bush. *Because I love it. Because growing things matters.* And growing them right—that mattered too.

"You can come work at the shop for me. You're good with transmission work—and small engines. We could add a new specialty."

"I'm n-not a mechanic; I'm a f-farmer. And it's n-not like you have enough w-work to go around." Because in the end, in Mike's shop? It always came down to not enough work to go around, and Mike had kids and a wife, and Jed only had himself.

"I think you should pray about it, Jedidiah. Maybe this is a sign."

"Wh-what?" Jed glared at his brother.

"This disease. The landlord dying. All happening at the same time."

The *fuck* it was. Jed loved his older brother—had damn near worshipped him at some stages in his life—but drew the line at accepting the idea that God randomly destroyed shit to prove a point. Not just because Mike thought he should "pray about it" and maybe "come work for me."

"I d-don't b-believe that's how the L-Lord works."

"Isn't for you to say, bro."

Lots of things weren't apparently. Jed stomped his shovel into the dirt and grunted. Had Mike's theology or his self-interest provoked that remark? And who was Jed to question his brother's motives?

"Isn't for you to say either, Mike."

Chapter Two

The Law Offices of Marty Sullivan occupied half of an office duplex on a rundown corner in Westfield. Connor winced inwardly as he fucked up pulling into the parallel parking on the street. He was worse than a teenager, rusty after years living car-free. He flushed, hoping no one had seen his disgraceful second approach, which left him in the spot, but running late.

Marty was an old family friend—he'd been Bruce's lawyer, and was now Scott's. Connor hoped, as he approached the entrance, that old loyalty would forgive a few minutes of tardiness. The broker next door had one of those signs like a clock, the ones with the hands you moved to let people know when you'd be back. The clock read twelve thirty, but it was half past one now and there was a woman standing in the entryway, knocking.

"You know where he's at?" She gestured to the door.

"No, sorry." Connor shrugged apologetically, brushing by her to let himself into Marty's suite.

"Figures." She scuffed her foot along the floor, scowling. "Thanks anyway."

He was still nodding at her when he pushed through the door to Marty's, and ran smack into a familiar face.

"Amanda!" He steadied his sister-in-law with one hand—or ex-sister-in-law. Were Scott and Amanda exes if the divorce wasn't final yet? "What are you doing here?"

"Ow, fuck, Connor." She rubbed at her forehead where she'd collided with his chin.

"You okay, Mandy?"

"Yeah. I'm fine." She ran a hand through her hair. "Since, um, since Bruce left you guys the farm, and Scott and I are still married,

I have to be here. God, I don't know why. So fucking awkward in there. I needed a cig."

Connor studied her expression—lines creased her forehead and dark circles hung like angry moons above her cheekbones. "I'm sorry things didn't work out for you and Scott."

She sniffled and nodded once, a sharp, tight motion. "Me too."

Connor glanced down at her hand where a diamond sparkled. Not the one Scott had given her. "You're getting remarried?"

She gave him a long, exasperated glare. "Yeah."

"I guess . . . Congratulations?"

She rolled her eyes and started packing her cigarettes against the heel of her hand. He opened the door wide for her.

Watching her walk away, he felt a strange pang he couldn't identify. There was no love lost between Connor and his brother, but he'd liked Mandy. She seemed brittle and cold now, not even the same woman he remembered. Maybe that was the price one paid for being married to someone like Scott. His brother had never been easy to live with, and he'd always liked his beer and his friends more than spending time with family.

Did Scott even consider Connor family anymore? Or was Connor adrift now—family-less, anchorless? Despite the years he'd spent trying to forget where he'd come from, the thought left him hollow.

"Mr. Graham?"

Marty's paralegal-slash-secretary had called Connor "Mr. Graham" since he was seventeen and had run errands for Bruce. She was seventy if she was a day, and proper as all get-out in her pinstriped suits and severe bun. In the years since Connor had been home last, her hair had gone from a steely gray to pure white, but aside from that, she hadn't changed.

"Hi, Mrs. Kennedy."

"Can I get you a cup of coffee? He'll be a few minutes—he's talking to Mandy's lawyer, and Scott is back there—" she nodded toward the hallway leading to the offices "—glowering."

Of course he was. All of Connor's life, Scott had been angry. Why should today be any different?

"No, thanks, Mrs. K."

Connor took in the ancient wood paneling and the worn carpet. A photo of a much younger Marty in uniform hung on the wall. The place was exactly how it had been when Connor was a teenager. How was it that coming home felt more like time travel than a couple hours by car?

"Connor," Marty called from behind him.

"Mr. Sullivan." Connor extended his hand for a shake.

"Terrible business, son. I'm sorry about your uncle." Marty covered Connor's hand with his own, wrinkled and age-spotted, as he shook it, a surprisingly sympathetic gesture from the gruff old lawyer.

"Thanks."

"Let's get to it. Come on. Kennedy, coffee."

"Yes, sir." Mrs. Kennedy stood up with a sharp nod.

The small conference room hummed with the buzz of fluorescent lights, and Connor sank gratefully into a soft leather chair as Mrs. Kennedy placed several cups and a coffee carafe in the center of the table, then marched out, easing the door shut behind her.

A few minutes later, Scott came in, red-faced and surly.

"Con." He jerked his chin at Connor in what might pass as a greeting between near-strangers. Connor swallowed back his resentment and stood, reaching for a handshake.

"Good to see you, Scott."

Scott sneered down at his hand and grunted, finally shaking it gingerly, like he was afraid he'd catch something. He all but wiped his hands on his jeans afterward. *God, what an asshole.* Connor straightened his shoulders.

When Amanda came in, she was followed by a young man in a well-tailored suit who gave Connor a curious glance. This had to be her lawyer. They both nodded to Marty and sat down without saying anything.

"I want to sell," Scott said. He glared over at Connor. "If you want to keep it, you'll have to buy me out."

Connor shook off the twinge of sadness at the thought of the farm belonging to someone else's family, and nodded. "Yeah, I want to sell too."

"Okay, that can be arranged, but any sale is subject to Mr. Jones's lease." Marty poured himself a cup of coffee and studied Connor over the edge. "I'm surprised you don't want to keep it. I know you lived on the property awhile."

In a world where there was money enough for him to own the family farm and expand his studio space to include a gallery . . . yeah, he'd want to keep it. But he didn't live in that world. He lived in the one where the money from the farm would cover the construction costs for the expansion. "Is Mr. Jones a potential buyer? I was over there yesterday; he seems to know the farm really well." Connor thought of the tense expression on Jed's face when he told Hannah about the disease in the Rancocas, and the way it softened when he mentioned the farm's Facebook page. He obviously cared about the place.

"He might be. How's the crop?"

Connor shrugged. "I'm no expert. Seemed okay."

"How urgently do you need to sell? I don't mean to sound all doom and gloom about the prospect, but this economy . . . with the land subject to a lease for another two years . . ."

"I'm not in a hurry. It would be nice to get started on the expansion on my place in New York, but I don't have any financial problems and I live well. It's not urgent."

Amanda cleared her throat.

"I'd like to get on it as quick as possible." Scott glared at his wife. "Since it seems it's going to affect my divorce proceedings."

"All right, I'll get it rolling. I have nothing else that requires both of you to be present. Scott, we'll cover how this affects your divorce separately." Marty stood up. "Connor, walk with me a moment."

Connor followed him into the hallway. As soon as they were out of the conference room, Marty asked, "How are you holding up?"

Connor flinched at the question. He didn't know how to answer. He was fine. Sad, but somehow it still didn't feel real.

"I honestly don't know." The words slipped out.

A dark expression clouded Marty's face for a moment. "I know in some ways Bruce was like a father to you. Take it one day at a time. You'll be okay."

"I *am* okay," Connor insisted, though thinking of Bruce that way, as a *parent*, twisted him up inside—a hot tangle of longing and rejection. "I guess it hasn't sunk in yet."

"You have someone?" Marty winced. "A young man or someone to be there for you when it does?"

Connor resisted the urge to tease the old man about inquiring into his relationship status. "I have my work. I have my friends. It's enough, you know?"

Marty made a dubious face. "Work doesn't keep a man warm."

"Spoken like a man who's never spent a day on a photo set."

"You're a smart-ass, son. But you know what I mean."

Connor nodded. "Thanks, Marty. I'll be fine."

"Scott . . ." Marty looked back toward the conference room. "I know he doesn't treat you like family anymore."

He never did.

"I'm just saying," Marty continued, "Bruce was a very close friend. And he'd have wanted you to have family. If you need to talk to someone, you give me a call, okay?"

"Thanks, Marty."

"All right. I'll call Jed Jones and let him know what's going on."

"I appreciate it."

Bruce was the kind of guy to make his own funeral arrangements, which suited Connor fine.

Had been. Fuck.

Scott had freaked out and tried to take control, but the owner of the funeral home had reminded him that Bruce had known better than anyone what he wanted, and had paid for it in advance. Connor had been relieved when Scott had given up trying to be in charge and just let it go.

They'd been born eleven years apart, and it might as well have been a lifetime for all they ever bothered to know each other. Scott had been everything small-town America reveres: a football star, local boy makes good—until he blew out his knee playing college ball.

Then there had been Connor—the shy, fat faggot. There was no football scholarship to pay his way through school, so he picked blueberries until he was old enough to get a job at Burger King, and then flipped burgers to pay for books. The art program at Westfield

State had been his ticket out of town, and when he graduated, he'd been both broke and determined. New York had beckoned, and he'd made Brooklyn his home.

And here he stood in the new cemetery, sweating in a suit too expensive for Blandford, staring at the hole where a minister had just prayed over his uncle. The town was a stranger now, though it had shaped him like nothing else. He hadn't just left town. He'd abandoned it, and he'd never looked back.

Scott and his friends stared at him—curious and disdainful. How was it that those stares could make him feel seventeen years old again? Bitter and lonely and completely lost.

"Connor!" a voice behind him called. A jolt of recognition—Bethany Tyler, round with pregnancy. A smile stretched across his face as she picked her way along the gravel path toward him. They'd been childhood playmates, even through the "girls are gross" years. Older now—and tired, with two little ones clutching her black maternity dress—she was beautiful in that glowing-pregnancy way. Out of habit, Connor tapped at his chest, the absence of his camera a heavier weight than the camera itself.

"Beth." He hugged her, and her belly bumped his own, provoking an awkward laugh from both of them.

"I wish you'd come home sometime when nobody died." She patted his shoulder and pulled away from the hug.

"This isn't home." The words came automatically. It's what he'd said to his mom when he left for New York. It's what he'd said to Bruce after Mom died. He'd said it so many times since leaving at twenty-two years old, he could almost believe that this place had no hold on him and never had.

Bethany's face crumpled a bit, but she soldiered on. "Where are you staying? Would you like to come over tomorrow? It's game night."

"At a bed-and-breakfast in Otis. Game night? You still do that?" He smiled at the memory—gin rummy with Beth and her sisters at her mom's Formica table. Beth's eyes glowing in triumph as she displayed her winning cards. There had been good times, even if they were hard to remember since he only came back, as she said, when someone died.

"You know it." She rubbed her belly and grinned. "Chutes and Ladders and Candyland with the kids, then after they go to bed, we play card games. It was poker for a while, but lately we're on a Cards Against Humanity kick."

"Who comes over?" The thought of seeing his old classmates filled Connor with dread.

"Hannah and Mike Jones usually. Some of Aaron's friends from the plant might come by with their wives too, but don't worry, Scott doesn't hang with their crowd."

Oh, thank god.

"Hannah Bradshaw-now-Jones? So she's not Jed's wife?"

Beth laughed. "No, she's his sister-in-law. I forgot she helps him at the farm. He sometimes comes too."

"No single gay men?" Maybe Kyle would be there, and they could catch up.

"The only one I ever knew moved to New York after college, so I guess you're shit outta luck." She slapped his arm. "Anytime after six. Say you'll come by."

"I'll come by."

"We bought the old Garten place, on Main Street. You know the house?"

God, of course he did. All these years away and he still knew houses by the names of the people who'd lived there when he was a kid.

"Yeah, I know the place."

"See you tomorrow, then!" She waved as she deftly maneuvered her offspring toward the parking lot, leaving Connor to stare after her, wondering what he'd just agreed to.

Chapter Three

The old Garten house—Beth's house—a seventies-era split-level on Main Street, glowed with strings of Christmas lights even though it was summertime. Yet the effect was festive, and not as out of place as Connor expected. Standing beside his rental car, he snapped a photo. Several vehicles lined the driveway; a few parked in the yard. Aaron's friends from the plant were here in force—and Connor probably had gone to school with most of them. He double-checked to make sure he wasn't blocking anyone in, and locked the car. Unease filled him. He wasn't great in big groups, and a group of people whose last memories of him were his awkward teenage years? Agreeing to come to game night had been a colossally dumb idea.

A child's squeal pierced the air and a small form hurtled out from behind the house and tumbled down the hill, rolling to a stop at his feet. A dirty face smiled at him, and the kid—A boy? Girl? With long hair and no shirt, who could tell?—grabbed on to his jeans and pulled to their feet, then raced back up the hill, shrieking again.

Beth appeared in the doorway at the front of the house and called down, "Hey, we're on the back porch. Go on around where Madison just went." She disappeared into the house, and Connor started up the hill, trying to find the part of himself that fit in here. It was like trying to put a shoe on the wrong foot—familiar and almost right, but uncomfortable and awkward. It was exactly the feeling that had sent him running to New York as soon as he had graduated. Did it matter if he was the foot or the shoe if they both rejected each other?

He followed the shrieks around back to find the porch lit by citronella candles and tiki torches. Faces flickered over hands of cards. On the floor, a game of Candyland lay abandoned, and out in the yard, six or so kids chased each other and fireflies. A wave of nostalgia hit him. Sure, there were fireflies in the city, but somehow, he'd hardened himself against caring about their early-evening show.

"C-Connor?" A soft voice called from behind him. He twisted to see Jed Jones standing a few feet away, a six-pack in hand and a tentative smile on his face. Hannah came up beside Jed carrying a plate of cupcakes. God, he hadn't brought anything, not even a bottle of wine. He knew better, and here he was perpetuating stereotypes of rude New Yorkers.

"Hi, Connor." She smiled. "Bethany said you might be joining us. It's nice to see you. Bruce's service was lovely yesterday."

"Thank you." Oh god, that was absurd. Thanking someone for a compliment on a funeral service self-arranged by the uncle he'd practically abandoned. Connor flushed.

Jed's lips twitched like he knew what Connor was thinking. He turned his attention to Hannah. "Mike changing diapers in the backseat again?"

She laughed. "Yeah. I promise he won't leave it in your car this time."

"Thank you." He nodded, then brushed past Connor, lifting the beer. "Gotta st-stick this in the cooler."

Connor watched him stroll up the back steps to Bethany's house to be greeted enthusiastically by the cardplayers. Jed's lanky grace was a compelling contrast to his stammer and silences. When a woman gestured for Jed to come sit by her, Connor forced himself to pull his admiring gaze away, and faced Hannah.

"Can I take those for you?" He reached for the cupcakes.

"And let you take credit for my culinary masterpiece?" She feigned shock, then handed over the plate. "Absolutely."

Just then, the chubby toddler from the farm trailer ran between them, buck naked and giggling. Connor almost dropped the cakes.

"Billy!" Hannah shouted and chased after him.

A bigger, brawnier version of Jed came around the corner, red-faced and carrying an armful of toddler clothes. "Billy!"

"I think Hannah's got him." Connor smiled at the newcomer. "I'm Connor."

"Mike." He grunted, giving Connor a once-over. "You're Scott Graham's little brother?"

"Yeah."

"Sorry for your loss."

"Thanks. You must be Jed's brother?"

"Yeah. I'd shake hands, but I can't be sure there ain't kid shit on mine. Damn diapers." He shook his head ruefully. "You got kids?"

"Um, no?" Connor was taken aback by the question. It's not like he'd ever seen the inside of the closet. Could there be a person in Blandford who didn't know he was gay? Not that gay men couldn't have children, but he didn't expect the town's perception of homosexuality to have changed any more over the years than the town itself had—and the town never changed.

"Huh. Well, if you decide you want 'em, my advice is to adopt one already potty-trained. Excuse me. Hey, Bill-y!" He followed his wife toward the shrieking children.

Up on the back porch, Connor handed the cupcakes to Bethany, who kissed his cheek, and joined the card game, accepting condolences and introductions with equal ease—which is to say none at all.

And it got worse.

Everyone remembered him, and treated him like one of their own, but he still felt like he was sitting at a table full of strangers. His memories of them were frozen in childhood—that guy won the third-grade spelling bee, and that girl once threw up in gym class— but they weren't kids anymore. And they knew *each other*. They laughed and teased with the familiarity of people who'd literally spent their entire lives together, occasionally jostling Connor and saying "Remember that time . . ." and all he could do was search his memory and nod.

Throughout the evening, he kept hoping Kyle would show. Someone he remembered fondly from his teen years besides Beth. But maybe Kyle wasn't friends with their old crew. Hell, maybe he'd even escaped, gotten out of town. Hope flooded him, a rush of warmth through his veins as he pictured Kyle living out-and-proud in a city somewhere—maybe Boston or even New York—dancing in gay bars by night and working an office job for some nice, progressive company by day. He liked that picture—he liked it a lot.

As the game wore on, he noticed Jed politely ignoring the flirting from the woman next to him. She'd lay a hand on his arm, and he'd find an excuse to reach for the cards or his beer. She'd flip her hair and lean close, and he'd shift his chair. It was subtle, nothing that would necessarily trigger suspicion in either the woman or the others at the table, but it caught Connor's attention. At one point, Jed's gaze flicked up to his, and a wry smile danced around his lips. Unlike the careful deflection toward his female admirer, the expression Jed gave Connor was warm, flirtatious—hell, even encouraging. He couldn't have been more blatant had he winked. But surely Connor was reading that wrong?

After a while, Beth herded the children inside and presumably to bed. She came back sometime later, smiling.

"They're out," she whispered as she took a seat next to Connor. "Sorry that took so long."

Connor nodded and asked the question that had been nagging him all evening.

"Hey, what ever happened to Kyle Bauer?" He glanced around the room. "Don't you guys hang out anymore?"

Silence fell across the table. Everyone grew really interested in their cards, and unease crept through Connor's gut.

What the hell?

Finally, Jed spoke. "K-Kyle shot himself in the head two years ago. Left a w-wife and th-three kids."

Oh fuck.

Connor didn't remember standing up and leaving the table, or the screen porch door slamming behind him. He just felt an overwhelming urge to get the hell away from all those people, their happy game, the cloying familiarity that wasn't, and the next thing he knew, he was pacing in the front yard.

"Hey," Jed called from behind Connor. "You okay?"

Connor nodded, but the nod changed into a shake as he sat on the front steps. "Yes. No. I don't know, actually."

"You want t-to talk?" Jed sat beside him, brushing their thighs together as if by accident. He didn't move away, just let his leg touch Connor's. It was a nice, comforting touch. Connor wanted to turn into Jed's body, bury his face in that slim shoulder, and howl out his pain. Of course he couldn't do that, because that's the kind of intimacy grown men didn't share unless they were lovers, and sometimes, not even then.

How was it that the death of Kyle Bauer hit so much harder than that of Connor's own uncle? Because Kyle's was suicide and Bruce's was a heart attack? Because Kyle's happened two years ago and he never knew? Or because Kyle left a wife and kids behind and Connor's family was so broken? *Wife and kids.*

"Did he leave a note?" Connor's voice was tight and raspy, even to his own ears.

"Nah." Jed shook his head. "Big m-mystery."

"Did you know him?" Connor searched Jed's face.

"Knew him well enough to know he was qu-queer." He shrugged, jutting his chin. "Not many people in town knew that."

"That doesn't make his life less valuable," Connor hissed.

"Didn't say it did." Jed shrugged again. "M-might make it m-more so. To s-some people."

Connor closed his eyes. "He wasn't my lover."

"Nope."

"We were friends. I guess I always hoped he'd come out too."

Jed snorted. "Not here. You th-think he could come out, sit in his family pew at the big white church, and face judgment from the closed-minded people in this town? You think K-Kyle fuckin' Bauer was strong enough for that?"

"You have strong feelings about what it takes to be gay in Blandford? Or maybe about who deserves to sit in that church? Christ, and people act like they don't understand why I left."

"Please, d-don't take the Lord's name in v-vain," Jed whispered. "I have a lot of st-strong feelings about that too."

"Of course you do." Connor stood and paced into the front yard again. "You drop the f-bomb like it was Kyle's middle name, and you're offended I said 'Christ.' I fucking hate this town."

"I'm not this town— Hell, half the t-time I hate it too. If you hate me, j-just say it."

Connor stopped short. "I don't hate you."

"D-didn't think you did."

"You confuse the hell out of me."

Jed cocked his head to the side and stared. "Why?"

"Are you gay?"

Jed wouldn't meet his eyes. "That's a c-complicated question."

Connor sat again, not caring if their legs touched. "There's nothing complicated about it. You like dick or you don't."

"I'm a Christian."

"The two aren't mutually exclusive."

"In th-this town? In my family? Yeah. They are."

"Bullshit. I was gay in this town. I don't know your family, but Hannah and Mike seem like good people. Would they treat you differently?"

"This from Scott Gr-Graham's brother?"

Connor didn't have anything to say to that, but Jed had his curiosity piqued. "Why are you telling me this?"

Jed snorted and looked away. When he spoke, his voice sounded tight, strained. "I was home-sch-schooled, did you know that? That's why you and I never met when we were younger. You must've w-wondered."

Connor *had* wondered. He couldn't take three steps in this town without seeing someone he'd gone to elementary school with, or someone who'd painted his face at the fair, or someone who'd picked blueberries for Bruce. "What does that have to do with it?"

"My parents say it was so we could have a r-religious education. I think they didn't want me to be g-gay. If I went to public school, with other boys, I might be tempted." His lips quirked ruefully, not quite into a smile. "I had a crush on John D-Denver."

"They homeschooled you because they thought it would keep you from wanting to bone John Denver?"

He chuckled and ducked his head. "It wasn't about b-boning. I just . . . I just thought he had the nicest smile. Don't you think he had the nicest smile?"

"No," Connor said softly. "I think you do."

Jed's smile faded, and he shook his head. "I d-don't know how to take a compliment from an attractive man. I don't know if you're f-flirting or just being nice. But thank you."

"You're welcome." Connor bumped their knees together. "You didn't answer my question."

"Be-because you remembered Kyle. He and I . . ." Jed shook his head again, exhaled slowly, then held out his hands as if in supplication. "K-Kyle. It would have been adultery. He w-was married."

"You and Kyle?" Connor could picture it, oddly enough. Yes, Jed was exactly Kyle's type. Quiet. Thoughtful. *Closeted.*

"I'd h-have gone to hell for that man. But n-no. Not while he was married."

His words hit like a punch. To have a love like that, and lose him? So much unsaid, but Connor could see naked grief on Jed's face.

"I'm so sorry."

"M-me too."

"You really believe that? That you'd go to hell for being gay?"

Jed dug the heel of his hand into his eyes. "Half of f-faith is d-doubt. I d-d-don't know wh-what I believe some days. I don't think being g-gay is a sin. Sex outside of m-marriage? L-l-lying? Adultery? Th-those are sins."

A firefly flashed just in front them, a flicker against the darkness of the front yard. Connor let his leg brush Jed's again, and he didn't pull away. Tempting as it was to wrap an arm around Jed and take some of his pain, Connor knew the gesture would be unwelcome. So they sat, tied together by their loss, until Hannah and Mike came around the corner, Mike carrying a sleeping Billy.

"Hey." Hannah smiled awkwardly, twisting her hands together. "Time to go."

Jed nodded and shot Connor a resolute glance. "Good night, Connor."

"Good night."

Following his brother and his sister-in-law to the car, Jed took one last peek over his shoulder. It was too dark to see his expression, but his tentatively raised hand was as good as a smile.

Jed handed his brother the keys, and watched Connor sitting on the steps until they pulled out of sight. For a big man, Connor appeared tiny in that despondent circle of light. Jed hated having to tell Connor about Kyle. Kyle had been *his*—what they'd had together had been beautiful, precious, and secret. But then, that was the problem wasn't it? Too many secrets ate away at a man's soul; Kyle was proof of that. The sharp ache of loss and blame ate at Jed. He'd been the one with the ultimatums and the demands, and if he'd known? If he hadn't pushed Kyle for *more*, where would they be now?

And that Connor Graham would come home, the town's own prodigal gay, and be welcomed with open arms? Jed shuddered, a bolt of loathing working through him, but whether it was aimed at himself or Connor, he wasn't sure. Everything he admired about Connor, he rejected in himself. He was jealous of Connor's out-and-proud lifestyle, and he resented that Connor had known Kyle first.

How dare he ask about Kyle, call him a friend, harbor these, these *hopes* for him—and stay away all those years when Kyle had *needed* people to love him?

But in spite of his jealousy, he had a bond with Connor now—another gay man here. Jed longed to connect with this stranger who knew more about him than his family did. That made it hard to hold on to jealousy.

"Okay, brother?" Mike glanced across the front seat at him.

"Just s-sad. Thinking about B-B-Bauer."

"Yeah. Can't believe he didn't know. Those two were tight years ago."

"He's n-n-not . . . n-not— Fuck." Jed glared at his brother, willing him to understand the words he couldn't seem to stammer out: *He's not one of us anymore.*

Hannah reached forward from the backseat and patted his shoulder gently. "Shhh, Jedidiah. Take your time."

"S-sorry for sw-swearing in front of Billy."

"Billy's asleep; he didn't hear anything."

"W-when he left. C-Connor. He didn't look back." Jed sighed at the relief of getting through the words.

"And it's like he forgot he was ever here?"

"Like w-we forgot too." Like the whole damn town had forgotten that one time the closet door opened.

Jed stared out the window at the darkened countryside around them; the trees, fields, and old houses loomed, so familiar. They seemed almost alive with their disapproval of his sudden desire to forget and be forgotten. To slip away from family and obligation, to find some little pocket of earth to cultivate somewhere free of the expectations of others. Was it really so wrong to covet the freedom that Connor had?

Hannah's hand found his shoulder again and gave it a squeeze. He was sure she meant to be reassuring, but for a brief moment, her touch felt like a restraint.

Chapter
Four

Since returning to town, Connor's dreams had been haunted by memories he'd buried ages ago.

The bleachers at the high school digging into his legs and someone saying, "If you want to play ball like your brother, you'll have to lay off the hot dogs." He'd woken up hungry and ashamed of it.

Bruce teaching him to skip rocks on the reservoir. He'd woken up with his throat tight from unshed tears.

His mom, not like she was when she was sick, but how she was when he was little—long hair tied back in a ponytail, and that smart blue waitress uniform she was always ironing. He'd woken up warm and happy.

Chasing Kyle through rows of blueberries, laughing and teasing each other, and when he caught him, a salty, blueberry-and-tears-flavored kiss, only it was Jed Jones and not Kyle, and this wasn't a memory, but it felt so real . . .

A phone ringing ripped Connor from this latest dream, dimly aware his heart was pounding like he'd run for miles. His pillow was wet with tears.

Blearily, he wiped at his face, and glanced at the caller ID—his agent in New York. Resolving to call him back when he was more awake, Connor sank back against the pillow and tried to remember the dream. Kissing Jed in his dream had been like kissing every lover Connor had ever had and none of them, his brain filling in the imagination with memories of what he liked. He built on that fantasy, calling up Jed's face just as his hand settled around his cock. He groaned at the pleasure slicing through him, a pang of lust and urgency. A few quick tugs, and he shot into his shorts, gasping Jed's name. *Ah fuck.*

He cleaned up in the shower, using the last of the small shampoo bottle provided by the bed-and-breakfast, a reminder he couldn't stay here much longer. He'd either need to go home to Brooklyn or find longer-term accommodations.

Still damp from the shower and wrapped in a towel, he called Peter back.

"Bitch, I called you an hour ago. I was about to call that British kid with the pompadour and offer him the job instead."

"Good morning, Peter. It's been twenty minutes, not an hour." Connor smiled into the phone. "The British kid with the pompadour is a lousy photographer, and we both know it. What kind of job are you talking about?"

"Spring lookbook for a menswear designer. They want something atmospheric. Rustic. Fog and trees and bare feet, but not a beard in sight. I'm over the beard thing, aren't you? Clean-shaven models. Like that kid you shot for Andrew Christian."

"Oliver Conklin?" Connor jotted the name down on a notepad on the desk.

"That's him. You know him pretty well; do you think you can get him?"

Good question. Connor had known Oliver for years through an artist friend, Jeff Kuyper. When Jeff died, Oliver had seemed a little lost, so Connor sent work his way when he could. Not often enough with the trends for beards and tattoos, neither of which suited Oliver's otherworldly beauty.

"Yeah, probably. He's twenty-seven years old though, hardly a kid."

"That old? Doesn't matter; he's right for this. Him, and maybe two or three others like him. The art director specified 'androgynous and homoerotic.' Goddamn, I'm getting hard just thinking about it. What do you think? Maybe someplace upstate?"

"Blueberry fields," Connor muttered, picturing two men embracing, just like in his dream but fueled by Peter's vision.

"I'm not sure I follow."

"I own a blueberry farm. Or, I do as of last week. It's like you said, rustic. I think it might work. I'll talk to my tenant and see which fields we might be able to use."

"Aren't you full of surprises? I can see it now. Oh, can you process the photos like an old cyanotype? We can call it 'Blue Boys' or something like that. What do you think? We can pay homage to one of the great magazines of our youth."

Peter continued to babble about how a high-concept editorial shoot was just what Connor's career needed right now, while Connor scribbled down the names of a few models he thought would work for the shoot, half listening—*Cyanotype? Yeah, I'll be talking him out of that one*—until Peter finally paused for breath.

"This sounds great," Connor interjected. "Call the usual agencies and have them send some guys by the atelier for casting. Do they definitely want Oliver?"

"If you can get a verbal, I'll get with his agency on details. Thank you, love. Let's firm up dates when you get back to New York. You are coming back, right?"

Homesickness struck him with a pang—for his apartment in Brooklyn, for the joy of his work, and for the simplicity of his relationships with his friends and colleagues.

"Yeah, I'm coming back."

"Okay, call me the second you get off the train. This shoot is going to be epic. Blueberries. You're a fucking genius."

"Yeah, thanks, Pete."

He hung up the phone and stared for a long moment at his notes.

Jed. He needed to talk to Jed about the location. He probably should have asked first, but it was so easy to get swept up in Peter's enthusiasm. Call Jed? No, it would be much harder to say no in person, and Connor wasn't above pressing the advantage. He'd drive to the farm.

He grabbed a pair of jeans and a button-down shirt, his go-to outfit for camouflaging his unfashionable belly. Why did he suddenly care what Jed thought of his body? Damn that dream. After talking to Peter about pretty-boy models, he couldn't help but feel self-conscious. He'd come a long way from that shy, chubby kid he was in high school, but deep down, that kid waited, always ready for the next snub.

No, he couldn't think like that. No one would be snubbing anyone. He was going to the farm to talk business, not flirt with his tenant. As attractive as Jed Jones was, he was closeted and seemed to have pretty strong feelings about casual sex. Nothing Connor had seen led him to believe Jed would have any interest in sinning with him. Remembering the jut of Jed's chin and the cut of his cheekbones when Connor photographed him at dawn, he couldn't help but think it was a damned shame.

On his way to the farm, Connor called Oliver, bypassing the agency booking and dialing his cell.

"Hello?" His voice was sleepy, and Connor could hear another voice rumbling in the background.

"Oliver, it's Connor Graham. I've got a potential job for you."

"Oh, fantastic." Oliver yawned around the word, drawing it out. "Another underwear gig?"

"No, menswear, and it involves travel. Want to come frolic barefoot in rural New England?"

"Mmm, yes, please—like a perfect summer getaway. The city is stifling right now."

"I thought you lived on Long Island with your sister?"

"I get my mail out on Long Island at my sister's house, but I'm living in glorious sin in the city at the moment."

There was a note of something wistful in his voice, and Connor recalled how a year ago he'd still been reeling over Jeff's loss. It brought to mind Jed, and the hollow tone in his voice when he'd talked about Kyle. Connor swallowed, fighting back the questions he wanted to ask, afraid they'd come out like accusations, when really, he was glad Oliver had found someone new.

"That's good, Ol. You sound happy."

"Yeah, I am. And I'm definitely up for the frolicking. Send my agency the details when you have them, okay?"

"Will do."

"Y-you're kidding." Jed stared at Connor, irritation flushing his face. He set down the two carriers he'd been taking to the barn for packing, and glared. "Here?"

Connor blushed, glancing down at his feet, then lifted his blue eyes to meet Jed's own. "I know I should have asked before I suggested it to Peter. I'm sorry. We'll pay you plenty."

Money would help, sure, but what if they damaged the plants? Jed pinched the skin at the bridge of his nose. Damn it, why couldn't Connor have just called? It would be easier to say no over the phone. He hated being put on the spot, and it didn't help that his landlord was peering through his eyelashes at him with a sheepish expression that could only be described as "adorable." It was like once the guy deduced Jed was gay, he pulled out all the stops and hit him right where he was most vulnerable.

"How long w-will it take?"

"Two days, maybe? A weekend." The sheepish look dropped. Now that they were negotiating, Connor raised his chin and met Jed's eyes directly. "And we'll keep the crew small."

Jed opened his mouth to ask how many, and Connor said, "A handful of models, a hair and makeup artist, a stylist, the designer's art director, and her assistant."

"W-where are they going to sl-sleep?"

Connor's face fell—clearly he hadn't thought of that. There weren't any hotels in Blandford, and Jed would be damned if he would let strangers sleep in his home.

"There's a bed-and-breakfast in Otis, that's where I'm staying. We'll reserve the other rooms."

"Rick's only got f-four rooms in the whole place."

Connor's shoulders slumped, and Jed felt guilty for bursting his bubble—like kicking a puppy.

"You're right. It was a dumb idea. I didn't think it through."

Well shit. Jed hadn't said that, and he hated the word "dumb." Why was he so dead set against this anyway? He'd seen how Connor had changed when he was behind the camera, how mundane things turned beautiful and fascinating when he drew attention to them. It might be fun to watch him work.

"W-wasn't dumb. Just not p-practical."

"Yeah. Sometimes the artist side of me leaps ahead of the business side. It's okay. We'll figure something out. If the art director is dead set on blueberries, we can always go to New Jersey."

"Y-you can stay here," Jed acquiesced. "Just y-you. No st-strangers."

"Really?" Connor's face lit up, then he cast a nervous glance up at the house. "I haven't been in the big house since Mom was alive."

"Hasn't ch-changed much. Some of Bruce's stuff is still in the attic."

"Thanks, Jed. I'll stay out of your way. And you know what, fuck it, the models can stay somewhere in a hotel and drive here. They get paid enough to deal with an early call."

Jed nodded and reached for the carriers. "W-when?"

"A few weeks? I need to go home and make the arrangements. August probably."

Jed nodded again. There would still be late fruit on the bushes, but the season would be drawing to a close. "J-just leave a message w-with Hannah when you know the dates."

"I will. Thanks."

"I'll stay out of your way." And what if that wasn't what Jed wanted? There was something—something beyond attraction—about Connor that put Jed at ease, made him feel more comfortable in his own skin than he'd felt in a while. He liked the way Connor didn't push him to speak faster or treat him like he was stupid because of his stutter.

Sure, he was coming in and out of Jed's life like there was a revolving door on it, but how often did Jed have a chance to spend time with other gay men? This might be his last chance before August.

"If-if you're here for a few more days, before you go back . . . w-w-would you . . ." He paused, taking a steadying breath. Connor waited patiently. "W-would you like to have d-dinner w-with me?"

Jed watched Connor absorb the question, a smile spreading slowly across his face, blue eyes twinkling. That sheepish look returned as he rubbed a hand over the back of his neck. "Yeah. I would."

Jed smiled, relief rushing through him. "I c-can cook."

Connor's face fell a bit. "You're in the closet."

"N-no. W-w-well, yes. But . . ." Jed paused again, waiting for his words. "Only restaurant in town's B-Burger King."

"Oh." Connor grinned, catching on. "Yeah. Dinner here would be nice."

"T-tomorrow?"

"What time?"

"S-seven?"

"It's a date."

Chapter Five

Connor drove to the package store before heading over to the farmhouse. The drive out of town just for a bottle of wine felt extravagant, but Jed probably didn't date often, so a little extravagance was worth it. He sent a quick text to Jed from the parking lot.

What are you cooking?

A moment later, the answer came back. *Meatloaf and mashed potatoes. Got a salad too.*

He chose a moderately priced Malbec—ignoring the dust on the bottle—and paid at the register that served both the takeout pizza joint and the beer, wine, and liquor sales.

"Connor Graham, is that you?" A woman in a white apron, covered in flour, came from the pizza side to greet him. She was older, more tired looking than he remembered, but familiar enough to bring a lump to his throat. He couldn't go anywhere in this town without encountering ghosts, but this was one he was happy to see.

"Miss Richards?" His high school art teacher, who had taught him so much about composition and light and how to make a career in the arts. "I can't believe it."

She smiled and flapped a hand. "Mrs. Poirot now. Celine and I got married once it was legal. No more closets for us. But call me Martha; I'm not your teacher anymore."

"No way! Man, I wish I could have seen the expression on Principal Carey's face when you came out. Congratulations. What are you doing working here?"

"Budget cuts. The school shut down the art and music programs. But this is close to home and I can paint in my off time. Connor, honey, I was so sorry to hear of Bruce's passing."

Connor's chest ached, for his own loss and for hers—god knew she had a passion for teaching. A teacher determined to see her students at their best, she hadn't only taught them technique, but also to question and contextualize so they could create with confidence. She'd given those rural kids, bussed in from seven towns, art. And she'd given Connor his dreams of something beyond Bruce's farm. There were days when he was certain she was the only reason he'd survived high school. "Thank you."

"So, where are you going all dressed up with a bottle of wine in hand? Hot date?"

He lowered his eyes a moment. How much could he say? He didn't want to inadvertently out Jed. Finally he just shrugged, met her eyes, and winked. "Couldn't say."

She nodded, grinning widely. "You're in town for all of a minute and you catch a date with a closet case? Boy, you got some game."

He laughed. "I don't think it's quite like that. More of a friend thing."

Her face sobered. "You know you do have friends here, Con. Not just family—and there's more of us out than you'd expect. You think you were the only gay kid who ever ended up crying in my office?"

"I don't want to drag it all up again, Miss—Martha. You know what it was like for me here."

"And it hurt my soul how little I could do about it. But that was a long time ago. We're a bit more progressive around here now. There are plenty of us who wouldn't mind seeing you more."

"Yeah, well, don't get your hopes up. I'm only here to sell the farm."

"And to bring a thirty-dollar bottle of Argentinian Malbec to a 'friend's' house for not-a-date?"

He cut her a little side-eye. "I didn't say it wasn't. I'm just not sure it is." He brandished the wine bottle. "And it's polite to bring a gift to your host."

"Yes, it certainly is," she drawled. "Have a good night, Connor."

His good mood lasted until he pulled up in front of the farmhouse, where Jed stood on the porch watching someone from the broker's office hanging a For Sale sign at the edge of the property.

Well, shit.

He grabbed the wine and made his way up the front steps, holding out the bottle like an offering. "Hi. I didn't know what you like, but red with beef, right?"

Jed glared at him, taking the bottle none-too-gently. "A h-h-heads-up w-w-would have been nice."

"Marty said he was going to talk to you."

"W-well, he didn't."

"I'm sorry." Connor held up his hands in apology. But why was he apologizing? Everyone knew why he was here. "If I'd known Marty was going to send someone out here to hang the sign before he talked to you, I'd have told you myself. I didn't want shit to be all awkward."

"G-guess w-what?" Jed gritted out through his teeth.

"What?"

"It's awk-awk-w-ward."

"I'm sorry. Truly, deeply sorry."

Jed scowled for a moment longer, and Connor felt like an ass, but he also felt defensive, stubborn. It wasn't like Jed was in danger of losing his home. Any sale would be subject to the lease, and he still had two years left. "Come on, man. I honestly didn't know."

Jed rubbed at his eyes, pulled his baseball cap off and fidgeted with it a minute, then slapped it back on his head. He studied Connor again, and whatever he saw must have satisfied him, because he nodded his head grudgingly.

"Apology ac-cepted."

"I wish it didn't have to be like this. I hate that the farm is between us, that we didn't meet in some normal way."

Jed cast another glance at the sign. "M-me too."

It turned out, Jed was a damned good cook. Sure, it was meatloaf, nothing fancy, but he'd spiced it well and served it with garlic mashed potatoes and a salad with blueberry vinaigrette dressing. He wasn't much for talking at the table, but Connor found he didn't mind. He wasn't the type of person who needed silence filled, and he appreciated the companionship. Every once in a while, Connor would catch Jed studying him over the top of his wineglass.

"What?" he finally asked.

"I'm n-not good with c-conversation."

Connor shrugged. "Company is nice, even without a lot of talk."

"I w-w-want to talk. I g-get fr-fr—"

"Frustrated?" The minute the word left his mouth, Connor regretted it. Jed slumped and sighed, his face turning red as he stared down at his plate.

"Th-that."

"I'm sorry. I shouldn't have interrupted. It was rude."

"It w-was," Jed agreed. "But every-w-one does it."

"I can't say I won't ever do it again. But I'll try my best not to."

"Thank you."

"Do you mind if I ask you about Kyle?"

Jed met Connor's eyes, swirled the wine around in his glass, and took a slow drink. "G-go ahead."

"How'd you meet him?"

"G-gay chat room. He w-wasn't married y-yet."

"He cheated on you both?"

Jed snorted. "W-we didn't make promises. But yeah. And after..." He paused. "He still w-wanted to hook up, but I c-couldn't disrespect his w-wife, shotgun w-wedding or no."

"Wow. That's fucked up. And you—I thought you said sex outside of marriage was a sin?"

Jed frowned. "I'm not a str-strong or a p-perfect man. But I draw the line at adultery. I t-told him if he w-wanted me, he'd divorce her."

Wow. Connor dropped his gaze to the table. He'd known a lot of married men who fooled around on the side, but he hadn't pegged Kyle for the type. Then again, he hadn't pegged Kyle for the married-to-a-woman type to begin with. How well had he really known anyone back in high school? It had been all posturing and jockeying for what limited social status was available to the decidedly out-crowd. And of the out-crowd, he was the only one *out*—and only because he was no good at hiding anything.

"I still can't believe he was married."

"W-what about you? Boyfriend back in the city?"

"No. God, no. I'm not exactly great boyfriend material. I travel. I photograph beautiful people and that leads to jealousy and uncomfortable conversations. I'm not celibate, but you know, I don't have a lifestyle that invites intimacy."

"Sh-shame." Jed smiled over his wineglass. "Intimacy is n-nice. I m-miss—I miss that."

Connor caught an edge of flirtation to that smile, and a bolt of lust lanced through him. The idea of fucking—or being fucked by—someone like Jed was captivating. Would he be quiet? Would he want to lead? What kind of face would he make when he came? Would he want to linger afterward and sleep together?

He took a deep swallow of wine to cover his sudden blush, then said, "Yeah, intimacy is nice."

"T-tell me about the beautiful people."

Grateful for the change of subject, Connor launched into an explanation of working with models. "It's a weird industry, fashion. Sometimes you get to work with someone who's clever and businesslike, but a lot of them are just awkward kids who figured out how to work their camera angles in exchange for love or money."

"Hmmm. G-good money?"

"For them or me?"

"B-both."

"Yeah, usually. I mean, I try to work mostly menswear, and the pay isn't as good as women's fashion, but Chri—" he broke off mid-word, remembering how Jed got uncomfortable with him swearing before. "I just have a hard time with the way the industry treats women. I feel like an asshole when a conversation with an art director turns to 'make her look depressed—or dead, dead would be better.'" He mimicked a certain art director from a jewelry company he'd worked with once.

"No!" Jed's eyes went wide. "No w-way."

Connor nodded. And that was far from the worst request he'd ever gotten working women's fashion. "It's gross. I hate it." He was surprised by the vehemence in his own voice. "Anyway. Menswear doesn't make me feel as much like an asshole. And the models are more my variety of eye candy."

"And everyone kn-knows?"

"That I'm gay? Not much reason to keep it a secret, is there?"

Jed huffed, a little defensive noise. "I w-wish it w-were like that here. Don't know w-why it should be anyone's business."

"It's *not*."

"But somehow, every-w-one makes it theirs anyw-way."

Jed felt his words hang heavy in the air, and almost regretted saying them. He knew people had gossiped—and worse—about Connor. Kyle had used Connor as the example of why coming out was such a bad idea. He'd ticked things off on his hands: bullying, fistfights, school suspension, getting kicked off the football team—it had sounded like Connor had been through hell and that was all anyone could expect from coming out.

"Yeah, they do." Connor glanced down at his plate. "But they don't get any piece of you that you don't give them."

"That w-what you said w-when they kicked you off the football team?"

Connor's mouth dropped open. "Where did you hear that? I was never on the football team. I tried out because Bruce suggested it, but I never wanted to play. I hated sports. Wow, the gossip mill must have been digging deep for that— Oh. Kyle."

"Oh," Jed echoed, his face growing hot.

"It was a long time ago. He might not have remembered the details so well."

"Or it w-was an easy excuse, w-with nobody around to contradict it." How often had Kyle twisted things to persuade Jed to keep their relationship a secret?

Connor shook his head. "Fear makes people act in strange ways."

"S-so I'm learning." And it had been Jed's demands that had left Kyle so afraid. The familiar grief and guilt lay heavily in his stomach.

They sat in silence until Connor changed the subject. "So, you said there's some of Bruce's stuff in the attic here? Anything cool?"

"P-paintings, boxes of photog-graphs." There was a barn full of farm equipment too, most of which needed to head to an auction block, but Jed would let Marty tell Connor about that stuff.

"I bet those are mine. Can I see?"

His excitement was catching. Jed grinned—what personal history had Connor left behind?

The pull-down ladder leading up to the attic was rickety, and the lightbulb was out at the top.

"N-no bulb," Jed called over his shoulder. He turned to see Connor checking out his ass. Caught, Connor shrugged, a wry little grin tilting up his lips.

"I have a flashlight on my phone."

"G-go ahead. I'll b-be right back."

Jed hopped down from the ladder, scratching the nape of his neck with one hand. He wasn't used to being scoped out like that at all, let alone openly. He could pursue something—sex for sure, maybe something *more*—with Connor if he wanted to. *But what* do *I want?* Sex would be fun, but complicated, especially with the conversation about the For Sale sign still mostly unspoken. Sex with someone you have a business relationship with is just bad news. He let his eye follow Connor's backside up the ladder before he went searching for lightbulbs. *Nice ass.*

Getting involved with his landlord was definitely a bad idea—but hell if it didn't feel like a good one.

When he returned and climbed the ladder, Connor was standing over a quartet of landscapes, the light from his phone shining on them.

"My senior class project in high school," he explained as Jed screwed the bulb into place and came to stand beside him. Connor switched off the flashlight and tucked his phone away. Jed's voice caught in his throat. The paintings were of the farm in each of the four seasons. His farm, Connor's farm, it didn't matter. There was love in those brushstrokes.

"They're not very good, but oils were never my forte." Connor picked up the canvas showing the farmhouse in autumn, with two majestic maples spilling red and orange leaves across the front steps.

"This is b-b-beautiful." Jed pointed at the stripes of color converging on the horizon—the crop gone, the rows of bushes showed a final glory before dropping their leaves. It was Jed's favorite time of year. Connor's depiction of spring highlighted the flush of white flowers, and summer showcased the heaviness of the fruit. The winter painting evoked the silence of a snowy night, the landscape transformed in a blanket of blue and purple.

Connor set the painting down with the others and covered them with a sheet. "Can you ship these to me in New York? I'll give you the address."

"Sh-sure."

Connor opened a box of photographs and a quick grin lit his face as he pulled the first one off the top. "I took this for art class junior year. My mom."

Jed studied the picture for a moment. Connor had clearly gotten those blue eyes and that winsome bow-shaped mouth from his mother, but there the similarities ended. She was stick-thin with cheekbones that could cut glass. Her skin seemed faded, like the photo had been left in the sun, though the other colors stayed bright.

"She's wearing a wig." Connor pointed at the lush blond hair spilling around her shoulders. "She loved that thing. She wore it long after she went into remission."

"She had c-cancer?" That explained the pallor.

"Yeah, that's why we moved in with Bruce. Mom had Scott when she was sixteen—no one knew who his dad was, and Mom wasn't telling. She married my dad a few years later, but she didn't have me until she was twenty-seven. My dad bailed when I was a baby—I didn't really know him, you know?—and it was just me and her and Scott. She got sick when I was a freshman in high school. She couldn't wait tables anymore after that—too much exposure to germs with her compromised immune system."

"So your uncle t-took you in?"

"Yeah. He was kind of an asshole at first, but not in a mean-spirited way. He didn't have kids of his own and suddenly had a queer teenager living under his roof, and a sick sister he was driving all over western New England for chemo and radiation therapy."

"W-wow."

"Anyway, this was the 'glamour shot' I took for her. She really loved fashion magazines, so I tried to make her look like a model."

"You d-did."

"Thanks. I love this photo of her. When she got sick again, it was hard, but seeing this reminds me of the good times. I think—I think that's when I fell in love with photography. Trying to capture all those happy moments." He dug a little deeper into the box and pulled out another stack of images. He flipped through them, then stopped suddenly, his smile disappearing.

"W-what?" Jed asked.

Connor stared at the photograph. A teenaged Scott, scowling at an impish, grinning Connor, and he felt a twinge in his chest.

"This was . . ." He took in a shaky breath.

"Con?" Jed reached for the photo and stared at it a long moment. "Cutie. How old were you?"

"Four or five." Connor ran a hand over his eyes, waiting for the sting, for the tears to come, but still nothing. The edges of his grief were there, clawing at him in a desperate bid for escape. "He hates me."

"N-n-no." Jed handed the photo back. "W-who could h-hate the kid in that picture?"

"I was always too much. I was so emotional and so *enthusiastic*. Him and Bruce, they were *men*." He deepened his voice on the last word. "They were always pushing me to be more stoic, more like them. When I loved something and I'd talk about it, they rolled their eyes at me. 'There he goes again.'"

The twinge in his chest became a dull ache.

"I channeled all my joy and passion into art and living and sex. I never wanted to be cold like that."

"Yeah." Jed wrapped his arms around Connor's waist, pressed him back-to-chest, as if he could sense the storm coming.

"And now Bruce is dead, and I'll never have his approval like Scott did. And I don't feel a goddamned thing." Connor snorted. "Sorry."

"For w-what?"

"'Taking the Lord's name in vain.'" Connor made air quotes as he said it.

"Shhhh." Jed grunted, clearing his throat. "Y-you feel something."

"I stood there, at his funeral, and looked around at Scott and his friends scowling at me, and it was like I was seventeen again. But instead of seventeen being awful like I remembered, it was just empty. I couldn't even muster up the emotion I get when I take a picture."

"Shhhh." Jed tucked his head onto Connor's shoulder.

"It's what he always wanted. Me to be like Scott. To stop being so embarrassing, to stop being so gay. To stop being so fucking emo all the time." Connor shoved the photograph away.

The sob wrenching from his chest shocked him, but Jed seemed ready for it.

"It's okay. It's o-o-okay."

Connor turned, the sobs coming freely now as the pain flared hot and white in his chest. He buried his face on Jed's slim shoulder and keened out from the raw, empty place inside.

"It's o-oh . . ." Jed was whispering, rocking Connor close. "All y-y-you had l-left."

"Why can't I just mourn him like a son should? Why do I have to be the *man* now?"

"You are, b-baby." Jed kissed his forehead. "M-mourning. And a m-man."

Another sob racked Connor, stealing the breath he needed to talk, but that was okay, because he didn't need to talk now that the floodgates had opened. The loss of control would have embarrassed him if those comforting arms hadn't been so understanding. He held Jed, and he cried for the brother who hated him. He cried for the uncle who'd done his best to love his sister's kids like children of his own—even when he didn't understand them. He cried for the mother he still missed, and the crushing weight of the hole Bruce had left in his life where his dysfunctional family used to be.

He sobbed it all out, and he didn't protest when Jed used his sleeve to dry his eyes or his nose, or when Jed helped him stand up and led him down the ladder. He let Jed settle him on the bed—on Jed's own bed—and he watched, breathing slowing to normal, then hitching in appreciation, as Jed changed his shirt with an apologetic smile.

"O-okay?" Jed sat on the bed next to him, and Connor nodded.

"Yeah." The sobbing had left him empty again, but a good empty: clean and open.

"Been a l-long t-time coming?"

Connor nodded. "You called me 'baby.'"

Jed snorted. "G-g-guess I did." A flush spread over his cheeks.

"I liked it," Connor whispered, hugging Jed close for a moment before letting him go.

"Y-you can stay here." Jed rubbed at his face. "I d-don't mean that as a come-on."

"You're living the life they wanted for me."

"W-what?"

"You. You're what they wanted me to be. You're tending the farm. You might be gay, but you're not out. You're quiet and stoic and nobody could accuse you of not being masculine. You're everything my family wanted for me to be."

Jed's lips quirked up in a smile. "I'm not qu-quiet on the inside."

Connor smiled back, but then closed his eyes as a wave of exhaustion washed over him. "I would love to spend a night with you, but tonight I think I need some time to myself. These feelings, this thing that just happened."

"I g-gotcha."

Jed held Connor's hand as he led him to the front door. "You w-want me to b-box it up?"

"The pictures and stuff?"

Jed nodded.

"That would be great. Thanks."

"Come h-here." Jed pulled Connor close and pressed him firmly back against the door. Anticipation fluttered in Connor. Yeah, the date had turned really weird, but it seemed like Jed wanted to end it on a happy note. He traced Connor's cheekbone with one finger, then slid his hand behind Connor's head and took the kiss.

There was nothing shy or hesitant about Jed's kiss. It was demanding, his tongue seeking entrance while his hand tightened in Connor's hair. At Connor's low moan, Jed pushed closer, rubbing their bodies together. His other hand stroked up to play with a nipple.

Need spread over Connor like a balm as he returned the kiss, wrapping his arms around Jed's waist. He pulled back and took a rough breath.

"God, you're fucking sexy," he gasped before burying his face in the hot skin of Jed's neck, biting and kissing while Jed stroked his hair. Jed tugged at his hair, and Connor kissed him again, deep and sweet. He spun them around so it was Jed pushed up against the door while Connor rubbed their hips together slowly, sensually. This time it was Jed who made a soft noise in the back of his throat and Jed who slid his hands down to Connor's waist and held on, not coming up for air until it became obvious that they were going to dry hump each other to orgasm if they didn't stop.

"W-want to g-go back upstairs?"

Connor slowed the circles he was making with his hips, put his hand on the door, and rested his forehead against his forearm. "I need a minute," he whispered.

"Just w-wanted to kiss you g-good-night." Jed ran his fingers through Connor's hair. "Didn't m-mean to . . ." He gestured between them.

Connor laughed, a short little bark. "God. I want this, right? I want you. I can't believe I'm even considering turning down that offer. But I'm kind of a mess tonight."

Jed just gazed at him, all warm eyes and soft smile, and pushed away from the door. "An-nother time."

Connor nodded, then kissed Jed lightly on the lips. No tongue, no hands, just a gentle good-night.

"I'm heading home tomorrow. I'll call you."

"T-text is b-better." Jed shrugged self-consciously.

"Right. I'll text you."

"G-good night." Jed opened the door for him, and Connor stepped out into the warm summer night, aroused and confused, but smiling. It had to have been the strangest date he'd ever had, but he felt soothed in a way he hadn't in years—how could he have forgotten how good it was to be held in a way that wasn't about sex? Though the kiss—that definitely had been about sex. He wasn't sure how or even *if* Jed reconciled his religious beliefs with his sex life, but there was no longer any doubt that the attraction was mutual.

Chapter Six

At church the next morning, Jed sat next to his mom, and when Hannah and Mike showed up with Billy in tow, he could tell it was going to be one of *those* days. Billy squirmed and tried to wiggle out of Hannah's grasp. Their minister was of the opinion that children crying in church was better than children absent from church, so there they were. *What a bunch of bullshit.* Sunday school had been church enough for him and his brothers back in the day. Jed held out his hand for a high five from the toddler, who grinned and climbed into the pew next to him. Billy was a demonstrative kid, and he immediately snuggled close to Jed.

The sermon was about Ephesians chapter five, and when the minister really got going about wives being subject to their husbands, Jed started to tune him out. He was a believer—he'd been coming to this church since he was Billy's age—but the current minister was a lot more conservative than the last one, and Jed didn't agree with the tenor of many of the man's sermons. Especially ones about marriage. It wasn't that Jed objected to the passage in the Bible—he couldn't rail against guys who'd been dead for centuries. He did object to a modern-day pastor who ignored that the world had changed. Same-sex marriages had been legal in Massachusetts for a decade now, and this guy hadn't once referred to wives being subject to their wives or husbands to husbands. And that wasn't even touching on the hundred years of women's rights movements Pastor Green openly ignored. Jed came to church for theology and philosophy—a life of the mind and spirit—but all he'd heard in recent years was a regurgitation of tired sermons that hadn't changed in decades.

Jed tried to recapture the awe he'd felt growing up and going to church. The sense of being loved unconditionally. He stared at the stained glass. It was the same. The smooth wood of the pew felt the same to his hand. The scents of human bodies and hints of incense and furniture polish were so familiar, if he closed his eyes, he'd see the church clear as day behind his lids. Whatever was missing was a part of him, and he wondered when he'd stopped feeling it. Had he felt it since Kyle's death? Not that he could call to mind. Perhaps in those stolen moments with Kyle *before* . . . ah, but that was blasphemy, wasn't it? Ecstasy and religion—where was the line between the two? Certainly last night, with Connor, he'd felt a lot closer to God than he had in years. Maybe ever. Guilt, now *there* was a familiar feeling. And not the one he'd been longing for.

When Billy started squirming and making noise, Jed jumped at the chance to take him for a walk outside.

The summer heat was cloying, but Billy didn't care so Jed didn't either. His nephew's company was easy, without the pressure to talk or the impatience adults showed for his speech. It was comforting. They collected rocks from the parking lot, each passing some rigorous testing process understood only by Billy, until Jed's pockets were heavy and his heart light.

"Jedidiah." The voice from behind took him by surprise. He hadn't thought they'd been gone long, but the service was clearly over, as his friends and neighbors were trickling into the parking lot, all making lunch plans. When he turned to face Scott Graham, it was with a flutter in his belly. *He knows.*

"G-Graham." He nodded to Connor's brother and reached for Billy's hand. The toddler stared up at Scott.

"My brother was out at your place last night."

Jed bristled. "So w-what?"

"So nothing. Did you get the feeling he'd maybe try to hold up the sale due to some sentimental attachment to the old place?"

Jed laughed, but it lacked mirth. "No, I don't think s-so." *It was a fucking date, you idiot.* "He asked m-me to send the rest of Bruce's st-st-stuff to him. Unless you w-wanted it?"

"No. I don't want any of that stuff." Scott recoiled. "The old man gave me whatever he thought I'd find useful when he was still alive.

I haven't got use for Connor's high school art projects." Disdain lined his features, his expression petulant and unfriendly. "Don't know why you bothered keeping it."

"Didn't seem right to g-get rid of it. Wasn't mine."

"It's not worth anything. It's not like my brother is Picasso," Scott sneered.

"You w-w-wouldn't know it if—if he were. Come on, Billy. Let's go find M-Mama."

He nodded his good-bye to Scott, frustrated by his inability to say something smooth and witty to put the asshole in his place. Scott Graham had a reputation as a drunk and a bully, and Jed tended to avoid him. He would have given anything in that moment to defend Connor to his brother. Connor, who was so fierce in his desire to live a life full of beauty. How could anyone sneer at that? And in spite of what Connor had said, Jed didn't find Scott stoic or manly. He found him sad and mean. Scott didn't deserve the admiration of the brother he'd hurt.

Where had this surge of protectiveness come from? He had felt the storm of Connor's grief, had wiped his eyes, and had kissed him. After holding all that intensity in his arms, Jed wasn't sure he was the same person he'd been the day before. He wasn't sure he wanted to be.

Back in Brooklyn, life was almost normal.

Normal—if Connor could forget the shape of a slim body under his hands, or the taste of Jed's mouth, or the way Jed had held him as he came apart.

To avoid thinking about *that*, Connor buried himself in work, making up the sessions he'd had to reschedule for the funeral and planning the shoot at the farm. Eventually, those plans led back to Jed. The way their date ended had left Connor self-conscious, so when mid-July rolled around and he needed to confirm the shooting schedule, he was glad to have an excuse to text first. When the return text came a few minutes later, he had to stifle a guffaw.

Call Hannah to handle that for you. Save the texting for dick pics.

So, they were good.

Hannah won't mind? he texted back.

Shit, don't send them to her, you pervert.

A few minutes later, when Connor was eyeing the phone camera, wondering if Jed was joking or not, another text came through. *She's happy to help you with the logistics. Save time in your schedule for another night in?*

Hopefully more than one. *Count on it.*

Hannah helped him arrange the shoot for the middle of August. Connor would come out a few days early to spend time with Jed. Should he extend an olive branch to Scott, see if his brother would meet him for dinner? No, better to let sleeping dogs lie. He could only take so much hostility in one lifetime.

The model lineup for the shoot had been finalized, and Connor was thrilled. Oliver Conklin in all his forever-young glory, as well as Sebby St. John, a tattooed British kid looking for a big break. Connor shot with St. John's agency enough to know his wild reputation and perpetually-at-the-edge-of-viral Instagram account. These photos might make a name for the kid—and that could only help Connor. A black kid from Atlanta going by the single moniker "Campbell" and a willowy blond named Steven with cheekbones that were art in themselves completed the lineup. It was a good group of models, all known as hard workers, each with a distinct look. Connor was beginning to get excited about the job too, to see the artistic vision Peter had set out, to get a feel for the shoot beyond the expected paycheck. He was following the art. And he loved it.

On a whim, he texted Jed: *The beautiful people are coming to town. I'm stoked. I can't wait for you to see the art we're going to make.*

Jed's reply came hours later.

I'm happy for you. Struggling tonight. Almost told Mike I'm gay.

Oh shit. Connor hadn't been good at being in the closet. It had only been a matter of time before he mouthed off to the wrong football player and was outed to *everyone.* But nobody was good at coming out. The anxiety, the trepidation: it was crippling. Jed *was* as good as closeted got—not that that was saying much.

You okay? What happened?

This reply took a while also. Connor ran through a million scenarios in his mind. Jed coming out and being accepted easily—

what were the chances? The town didn't seem much different from when he'd left—he didn't have to look any further than Kyle's suicide for proof of that. Which he hadn't even *known* about before Jed.

I'm good. He started into me again about some girl he and Hannah want to fix me up with—and I've always gone along with it before, but I'm so tired of lying. It's not ever going to stop unless I figure out how to come out. I wish I could call you. I wish I could talk like a normal person because this is all up in my brain and I'd really like to know what you think.

Connor took a deep breath. He knew the phone was a no-go for Jed. It was the only reason to pay Hannah a salary for office work Jed was capable of handling on his own. Bruce always had.

Write me a letter. Take your time. ConnorGrahamArt@gmail.com.

Minutes passed. An hour. Then his phone and his computer beeped at the same time.

He opened the email and started to read.

Dear Connor,

This is weird, but it was a good idea.

I've known I was gay forever. I dated women and felt guilty. I hooked up with men from chat rooms, but never felt like any of them were men I wanted to make a life with. Until Kyle, because he got it, you know? He was like me. Rural. Red, but educated. I had a fantasy, like you do with your first love. Forever. We'd come out and take the world on our terms. But he didn't have the same plans. He didn't dream about owning a stretch of land and making things grow, least of all us. Nothing grows in the dark, Connor. After he died, I felt like I'd been betrayed. I'd been given a chance to have what everyone else gets to have, but my relationship was broken. Defective. Suddenly, coming out seemed like it would hurt people. Kyle's wife and kids. My parents. Me.

When you came home, you were so freaking normal. You weren't broken at all. You were grieving, and that was sad, but you were so bright and strong, and I wanted to be like you so much I resented it. I mean, I wanted to do you too. But it's like that, sometimes, when you admire someone the way I admire you and the life you live. I don't want to keep myself a secret.

I wasn't wrong, though. Nothing grows in the dark, but too much sun, too fast, can burn. Coming out will *hurt. It'll hurt me. And it'll hurt my family—they'll know I lied to them. I want to believe they'll accept a gay son, a gay brother. They're good people—which is why I don't know how to ask forgiveness for lying to them. Because I did. I slept with women, and that was wrong, but that kind of sin of the flesh? That's acceptable. The flesh is weak. The lying, that's a choice I made.*

And I don't know how to do this. I don't know how to hurt the people I love. Help me.

Jed

Connor took a deep breath and read the email again before he picked up the phone.

"H-hello?" Jed sounded scared and maybe a little annoyed.

"You don't need to say anything," Connor reassured him. "But I need you to hear my voice, to know how I'm feeling when I say this to you. You did nothing wrong. You didn't lie to hurt anyone. You protected yourself. Coming out is personal. And it's hard. It's so goddamn hard. Fuck. I'm sorry. I know how you feel about that. Jed, you're amazing. You've done nothing wrong. You don't have anything to apologize for. And you can't make this about them. Coming out is about you, about doing this for yourself. And yeah, it hurts. But using your plant metaphors, it's like cutting a bush to help it grow. I don't know the technical term."

"Pr-pruning." A soft chuckle.

Relief swept over Connor. "Okay, so you feel me? You don't have anything to apologize for. And, damn, I admire you too. *And* I want to do you. Okay, I'm gonna hang up now because otherwise I'm going to have phone sex at you instead of with you, and that's just weird."

He hung up; his phone buzzed.

Thank you.

He held the phone to his heart, eyes burning. Then he replied, *You're welcome.*

Chapter
Seven

Connor pulled up to the farmhouse just as the sun was setting and his heart gave a little lurch when he saw the dually parked out front. Hannah had said Jed would be home, but it wasn't until that moment, when he saw the truck, that he realized how much he'd anticipated seeing him. The science story he'd caught on NPR on the drive out here had only heightened his excitement.

He pulled his suitcase from the trunk of the rental car and took the steps two at a time to knock on the door. Tapping his fingers on the side of his leg, he stared at the chipped, flaking paint should he have it painted for Jed? Wasn't that the kind of thing landlords did?

The door swung open, and Jed's smile greeted him.

"Hi." Connor was grinning like a fool, but he didn't care. "Guess what? Tonight's the peak of the Perseid meteor shower, and we're going to watch it."

"W-we are?" Jed grinned back. "W-welcome home."

"This isn't—" Connor paused. No, it wasn't. But it was Jed's home. "Thanks."

"M-meteor shower?"

"I haven't seen one since I moved away from here. You forget things like this when . . ." Connor paused, looked at Jed, and willed him to understand. "When you move to a different world."

Jed stared at him for a long moment, his face growing solemn. He nodded, held the door wide, and reached for Connor's suitcase.

"I can carry my own suitcase."

Jed smiled again. "Of c-course. J-just being polite. G-guest room is at the top of the st-stairs."

"Thanks." Connor brought the suitcase upstairs and opened the door to the room that had been his, his last year of high school. He tossed the suitcase on the bed and glanced around. The room had been painted recently, bright white. A bit of the smell lingered. Blue flowered curtains framed the window, and a matching comforter covered the bed. In the corner, a crib stood, the sheets stripped off the little mattress and folded on top.

"M-Mike and Hannah stay sometimes after g-game night." Jed's voice came from behind him. "Billy drew on the w-walls."

"Oh." Connor glanced around the room again, and a low chuckle escaped. "He wasn't the first."

"That was y-you? The mural in the bathroom? I should have guessed."

Connor nodded. "Is it still there?"

Jed shook his head. "P-pipe burst."

A pang of disappointment hit him. He'd painted an octopus's garden on the walls around the tub. Bruce had called it "ridiculous" and "a waste of time," but had left it. Connor always wondered if Bruce had kept the mural because it reminded him of Connor or because of the Beatles song.

"I l-liked it." Jed smiled. "W-was sorry to see it go."

He stepped past Connor and into the room, crossed to the closet, and pulled out a box. He held it up to show Connor the contents. A camping mattress, twin-sized.

"For the t-truck. We c-can watch the meteor shower on it."

A lump formed in Connor's throat. He'd have gladly laid on a blanket on the ground, but this was *nice. Intimate.* He smiled at Jed. "Thanks."

Jed blushed and gave a little wave, then left Connor alone in the room.

Somehow, Connor had expected more. A kiss? A hug? But things were still so new, and Jed was a quiet guy. Connor really hoped they'd make up for it later.

It was midnight when Connor knocked on his bedroom door, but Jed wasn't asleep. He'd spent the evening tossing and turning and thinking ahead to the meteor shower, and back to one blisteringly hot kiss weeks before. The air mattress in the back of the truck wasn't very wide—he hoped it was obvious that he wanted to pick up where they'd left off. What would it feel like to touch Connor, to run his hands over that big body? Would he have chest hair? Jed imagined he would. He shoved his feet into his shoes and opened the door.

"Hey," Connor whispered. His hair was all tousled and his feet bare—clearly he'd managed some rest. But he was grinning like a kid in a candy store now, and his excitement was catching.

"Hey," Jed whispered back. "W-why w-w-whispering?"

Connor shook his head, but didn't stop whispering. "I don't know. Because it's nighttime and I feel like I'm sneaking out to see a boyfriend. Let's go."

Jed led Connor down the stairs and through the front door, then drove them along a bumpy dirt road to the center of the farm. There, he turned off the engine, grabbed the blankets he'd piled in the backseat, and climbed into the bed of the truck, shoving aside the straps holding the mattress in place. Connor joined him, smiling nervously as they lay down side by side on the mattress. It was a narrow squeeze, their shoulders brushing slightly. Jed tried to give Connor a little more room, but then Connor gazed at him, all serious, and Jed froze.

"It's a good thing you're skinny." Connor patted his own belly. "This wouldn't work if you were built like me."

"I l-like the w-way you're b-built."

Connor's surprise was etched clearly on his face. "You do?"

A hot blush crept over Jed's skin, and his cock started to harden. His stomach clenched with nerves, and his heartbeat rushed in his ears, but he reached out anyway. "I like th-this." He ran a hand down Connor's barrel chest to rest on his stomach. "You're manly."

Connor snorted, then laughed, his belly shaking under Jed's hand. "That's probably the first time anyone in this town has ever used that word to describe me."

But he didn't push Jed's hand away, and he sort of half dragged Jed closer, wrapping an arm around his shoulders so Jed snuggled to his side. It felt so comfortable, so *right* to hold on to Connor while they stared up at the stars. Jed wanted to close his eyes and remember this feeling forever. Like the bed of his truck on this night, in this place, existed out of time, and he was free to touch another man and nobody, least of all the man in his arms, could make him feel ashamed.

"You smell good," Connor murmured against his hair.

Jed flushed all over. "Th-thanks."

"The mattress was a good idea."

Jed nodded against Connor's shoulder, then turned his face up to see Connor. Who was watching him with a bemused expression.

"You and Kyle? You ever do anything like this?"

Jed shook his head. As if Kyle would have risked being caught cuddling another man in the back of a pickup in the middle of the night.

"What about your other boyfriends?"

"I *d-date* girls," he whispered. "D-don't know any gay men." Which wasn't entirely true. There were the guys he'd met online and then hooked up with, but with the exception of Kyle, he wouldn't call any of that *dating*. And even with Kyle, it had been a secret.

Connor raised an eyebrow. "Are you bi?"

Jed shrugged. "J-just lonely some. N-need to touch someone, be touched."

Connor nodded, like he understood, and Jed was relieved. Guilt about sleeping with women had haunted him, but something in Connor's expression felt like absolution. He ran his hand from where it rested on Connor's belly up to cup his face. So easy to draw him close and press their mouths together, his eyes drifting shut with Connor's smile filling his vision.

The kiss was lazy and gentle, sweet and slow—as different from their first kiss as two kisses could be, but the heat was there all the same. One of Connor's hands cradled the back of his head, the other rested on his chest, holding him, but not in a forceful way. Firm, mobile lips nibbled against Jed's own, playfully. But he wanted more. He opened his mouth and licked at Connor's lips, entreating, and lust rushed through him when Connor groaned and tangled their tongues.

Connor's body rolled against his, and the press of a hard cock against his own made Jed shudder. *Incredible.* The rub of their bodies, the heat of arousal building, it was so good, so *damned good*. A hand snaked up under his shirt, fingertips rubbing gently over a nipple. He threw his head back with a gasp and his eyes sprang open. Connor leaned close and nipped at his earlobe, and Jed saw stars.

With Connor's hand under his shirt, and mouth against his neck, and their hips thrusting together, it took Jed a moment to realize he was seeing the meteor shower, and Connor was missing it. With a stab of regret, he pushed Connor away from where he'd ignited Jed's skin with stubbly kisses.

"It's st-starting."

"Hmmm?" Connor sat up.

"Your m-m-meteor shower. It's starting." Jed pointed at the sky.

Connor growled and flopped down next to him, chest heaving. "You want to watch?"

Jed glanced over at him. "Y-yeah. B-but don't w-want to stop either."

"Come here." Connor sat up again, his upper body against the cab of the truck, and pulled Jed between the V of his legs. A hard cock rested against his ass, and a big hand maneuvered him back to rest on Connor's chest. "Gonna touch you while we watch, okay?"

Jed nodded and kissed Connor over his shoulder. Connor indulged him for a moment, then broke the kiss and gently turned him around.

"Watch." Connor's breath ghosted along his ear.

So he watched.

For a long time, Connor simply held him, every once in a while rubbing a hand across his chest or hip. Fingertips plucked his nipples through his T-shirt, and once the heel of a palm pressed against his dick. His whole body grew hot, his skin tight. When his eyes drifted shut and his head lolled against Connor's shoulder, Connor nipped his earlobe and murmured, "Watch."

This time, Connor's hands were more aggressive, kneading the skin of his chest and pinching. He couldn't remember the last time he'd been this aroused.

"Con-Connor, please," he whispered, and Connor angled his head and kissed him deep and hard. When they came up for air, Connor's roving hands stilled.

"Jed, I didn't come out here to pressure you into sex."

"I kn-know. W-we can, though, if you w-want, hell, anything you want. No p-pressure." Jed straddled Connor's lap and ran his hands up inside his shirt. *Oh, yes, chest hair.*

Connor grabbed his wrists through the fabric. "I didn't bring anything. Did you?"

Disappointment washed over him. "N-no."

"Okay." Connor kissed him again, nice and slow. "Turn back around."

Jed obeyed, and Connor's hands slid into the waistband of his sweatpants. One hand closed around Jed's cock and slowly stroked while the other cupped his balls. He was so aroused that his hips immediately started to thrust up, and Connor sped his stroke.

"So fucking hot, Jed. I want to make you feel good."

"You d-do." Jed gripped his own nipple, twisting a little through his T-shirt.

"Yeah?" Connor bit at his earlobe. "I'm gonna remember you like that."

Jed groaned as the rush of orgasm started to build, his balls drawing up tight. He twisted in Connor's arms, needing to be closer, needing more intimacy, *needing* . . . Jed shuddered, the pleasure rippling through him like a flash flood, overtaking everything at once. Connor's lips closed over his as he came, softening his shout with a kiss. He clung to Connor and stuttered wordlessly.

"I got you. I got you," Connor whispered against his lips, slowing his hand on Jed's cock until Jed pushed it away.

"You?" Jed aimed a lazy smile at Connor, reaching for his pants.

"I like this." Connor tugged Jed down with him so they lay on their sides on the mattress, facing each other. He pulled Jed into a loose embrace, hoisting one leg around his hip. It took a minute of rocking together before Jed picked up his rhythm, but when he did, Connor's breath immediately grew raspy. "Yeah, just . . . yeah." Connor gripped Jed's ass in both hands as he ground them together.

Jed watched his face, looking for that moment when Connor's eyes dropped closed and he gasped Jed's name. When it happened, a little thrill ran through him at the sight. Was there anything that made him feel wanted like making another man feel that good? Cum soaked the layers of clothing between them, sticky and warm, but Jed didn't care. He held Connor close and kissed him until Connor's breathing steadied.

"Did you see the stars?" he asked when Connor grinned and kissed him right back.

"Yeah, I saw stars all right."

Jed blushed. "Wasn't what I meant."

"I saw those too, but watching you come was more fun."

"Shameless."

"That was . . . It was awesome. Hey, you're not stuttering."

Jed nodded, tucking his head under Connor's chin and yawning. "I don't so much, when I'm relaxed. G-gonna fall asleep out here if we don't get back."

"Then we should get back."

The drive to the house didn't give Jed nearly enough time to figure out what to do next. Would it be weird to invite Connor to sleep with him? Was that too intimate? Would he come across as needy? Did he care? His indecision stayed with him all the way into the house, but then at the guest room door, he grabbed Connor's hand and gave him a quick kiss that turned into a slow, lazy grind up against the wall. When his cock started plumping up in his sweats, he pulled away regretfully. "I w-w-work early. Th-thank you, f-f-for tonight."

Connor smiled. "Yeah, back atcha. Good night, Jed."

He hesitated a moment. "D-do you w-want to sleep w-with me?"

Connor rubbed the nape of his neck and glanced into the guest room, then back at Jed. "Yeah. I do. Is that okay?"

"I'm up at f-five."

"That's three hours from now."

"Y-yeah."

Connor shrugged. "So worth it."

After years of secrets and sneaking around, denied this sort of intimacy even by Kyle, Jed had to agree. It was *definitely* worth it. So for the first time in his life, Jed took another man to bed with the intention of waking up next to him—and it felt damn good.

Chapter Eight

Jed stood back and watched Connor work with something like awe.

He wasn't sure what to think of the models. The oldest one—a dark-haired, blue-eyed guy—seemed awkward and uncomfortable, which wasn't how Jed had ever pictured fashion models. He stood over a black kid, his hand on the other man's hair, a pout twisting his lips. With the setting sun behind them, the sky shone like it was on fire. It was a striking scene, but Connor was shaking his head.

"No. Nope, can't do it. Campbell, trade places with Oliver. I don't like the racial connotations of having a black man on his knees in front of a white man—in a field. Jesus." Connor ran a hand through his hair and glanced over his shoulder at Jed. "Sorry."

Jed shrugged. He felt like an interloper, and he needed to get back to the barn to make sure the berries were packed and ready for the truck, but he couldn't help but steal a few minutes to watch the shoot.

The whole dynamic changed when Oliver got on his knees. Where it had been strained before, suddenly the air was charged with a raw sexuality. Oliver made a small noise, his eyes widened, his lips fell open, and the other guy, Campbell, smiled down at him like a benevolent god.

"Hell." A tattooed model with an unlit cigarette hanging from his lips came up beside Jed. "That's fucking sex right there."

Jed laughed, but his dick was half-hard. No wonder Connor said his job led to jealousy issues.

"Ollie, mate, save some of that for me," the tattooed guy catcalled, fumbling with a lighter as he leered.

Connor grinned over at him. "Sebby, put your tie on and get in the shot."

The model winked at Jed. A woman came up to Sebby and helped with his tie, taking the still unlit cigarette from his hand, and then he joined the shot. While the other men were in suits, he wore a deep-purple sweater, steel-gray trousers, and no shoes. Even his hands and feet were tattooed.

"Put your right arm around Campbell, and lean close like you're whispering in his ear, but look at Oliver when you do it. Tilt your left shoulder out more. Cross your right foot in front of your left. Good. Candace, fix his sweater."

The woman who'd straightened Sebby's tie ducked in behind him and did something to the back of his sweater that made it pull tightly across his chest, then slipped out of the shot again.

Click. Click. Click. A huge light flashed every time Connor took a picture, punctuating his movements. He was sweating, his T-shirt turning dark on his chest and back, as he moved about the set, giving directions to models and crew in even tones. His obvious competence, his take-charge attitude, it was all undeniably sexy. Jed was mesmerized, watching him.

"Enough for now, that's the last of the light." Connor lowered his camera to his chest. "Nice work, guys. Hell, Oliver, I think you even gave Steven a boner."

Campbell and Sebby were helping Oliver to his feet, and they were laughing. A blond model—Steven?—glanced up from his phone and flipped Connor the bird before he went back to texting.

The casual references to boners and sex were stunning and thrilling to Jed. It was teasing, but there was nothing mean-spirited about it. It was just guys poking at each other. And in Sebby's case, a lot of over-the-top flirting with the other models—and with Connor. A sharp stab of longing punched through Jed. What would it feel like to be included in their easy camaraderie? Of course, he'd have to be out, first. As far as they knew he was just another straight redneck.

"Jed?"

He'd been so lost in his thoughts, he didn't notice Connor approaching him.

"S-sorry. W-w-was w—"

Connor kissed him, a quick hello kind of kiss, but a kiss all the same. In front of the crew, the models, everyone.

Panic sliced through him, and he shoved Connor back. "D-don't!"

Jed peered around to see if any of his employees were nearby. They shouldn't have been, they'd been instructed to leave the shoot alone, but what if someone had come searching for him?

"Your people aren't here," Connor whispered. "And my people don't care."

Jed glanced around again—they were alone—relaxed a little, and risked a brief kiss back. He was rewarded by one of Connor's smiles.

"Want to see some of the shots?"

Jed nodded, and Connor held up the camera and let Jed scroll through the photos. They were hot. The photos from earlier in the day had a more subdued energy to them, but the ones he'd taken just now were decadently masculine and erotic. Jed had seen the phrase "suit porn" on the internet, but he hadn't actually gotten what it meant before.

"B-beautiful. This g-guy." Jed pointed at the last photo, Oliver on his knees in front of Campbell and Sebby. "He's g-gay?"

"Oliver? Oh yeah. Sebby is pansexual. Not sure about Campbell."

"W-what's p-pansexual?"

"Men, women, nonbinary . . . he loves everyone."

Jed was pretty sure the word "loves" was being used euphemistically.

Oliver came up behind them and slung an arm over Connor's shoulder. "Can you send me a copy of that one? Henry'll fucking love it."

Connor nodded, not looking up from the screen.

"Hey, you the farmer?" Sebby approached them. When Jed nodded, he continued, "You know if there's a queer bar anywhere around here? Would love to dance off some of this energy."

"No bars at all. Not unless you w-want to drive to another town."

"Henry will drive if I ask him to," Oliver piped up. "Loves to watch me dance." He swiveled his hips and bit his lower lip. "You in, Con?"

Connor glanced at Jed, a question in his eyes. Jed shook his head the teensiest bit. He told himself it was because he had work to do in the morning, and not that the thought of being seen at a gay bar—even by strangers—terrified him.

"Nah, I think I'll stay in." Connor turned to Oliver. "Want to get these processed and sent over to Peter for feedback before we get back at it tomorrow. Call's at 6 a.m."

"Your loss, babe." Sebby grinned at him. "I'm even better on the dance floor than in front of the camera. Ollie, let's go get your man and get our dance on."

Oliver laughed, and the two of them walked away, arms around each other's shoulders, while Sebby made *oontz oontz oontz* dance music noises. One by one, the other models wandered over and said their good-byes, while Connor and his assistant started breaking down his equipment. Jed gave a little wave, climbed into his truck, and headed back to the barn.

Hannah was waiting for him.

"The truck is here. Is everything ready to go?"

Shit.

"Let me double-check."

He should have been here a half hour earlier, but he'd been so transfixed by the sight of Connor at work. This attraction, it was turning into something else—a preoccupation, a fixation. He was letting it interfere with his work. He couldn't have that. As much as he admired and wanted Connor, and heaven knew he did, those stolen moments proved one thing for certain: they might have come from the same place, but they lived in different worlds now.

He made one final inspection of the cases of berries, all carefully packaged and labeled with the farm's info and organic certification sticker. He nodded to Hannah.

"Yeah, send him back here, then go ahead home."

When the truck was loaded and the cargo signed for, Jed followed the well-worn gravel path to the farmhouse, trying to find the resolve not to let his infatuation interfere with his work again. But when he saw Connor waiting for him on the front porch, camera in hand, grin on his face, it was hard not to answer with one of his own.

"Hi." Connor stood up as Jed approached with his hands in his pockets and glanced from side to side as if checking to be sure they were really alone.

"Hi." Jed stopped a few feet from the porch. "Y-you could have g-g-gone w-with them."

Connor's heart did a funny spinny thing in his chest. Did Jed not want him there? "Why the hell would I want to spend my time driving to Northampton to grind on some stranger when I could be with you?"

Jed snorted and squinted at the darkening horizon instead of meeting Connor's gaze. He didn't speak for so long, Connor wasn't sure he would answer the question at all, but when his answer came, it was surprising.

"I d-don't know why you'd w-want to be with me w-when Sebby would totally . . ." Jed swallowed, his Adam's apple bobbing in his throat.

Connor wanted to drag him inside and trace that Adam's apple with his tongue. Jed clearly had no idea how much he turned Connor on. How on Earth Jed could be jealous of a guy like Sebastian St. John was beyond him.

"Sebby would. I wouldn't. Seb is . . . He's funny, and charming, and that British accent is cute. But he's a train wreck. The stories they tell around his agency? He's got this on-again, off-again boyfriend who is way more successful than he is. They live together and fight like cats and dogs whenever they're in public. It's an epic shit-show. And I don't know which of them I feel more sorry for." Connor stepped down off the porch and stood toe-to-toe with Jed. "I want to be with you because I like you. And I think it's kind of sweet that you're jealous."

"I'm n-n-n— *Shit.*" Jed shook his head. "I g-guess a little."

"Should we go inside?" Connor gestured toward the porch. "Finish this conversation someplace where I can show you how much I'd rather be with you?"

The smile Jed gave him, caught between bashful and turned on, made Connor's breath quicken.

"Please?" he added.

Jed nodded and led him up the steps.

Once the front door of the house had closed behind them, Connor pushed Jed up against it and kissed him hard. Jed's lips parted on a moan and let him in. He tasted like blueberries, and a little like sweat. Connor grunted and stepped in closer, grabbing Jed's leg and pulling it up, around, so he could grind their hips together. Something about the taste of sweat on a man's skin turned him on like nothing else. He dipped his head to lick the saltiness under Jed's jaw, to nip at the side of his neck, and then, when Jed groaned low in this throat, Connor kissed his Adam's apple and hummed into the vibration.

"F-F-fuck."

Connor smiled, rubbed his hips against Jed's again, and then kissed his chin, his cheekbones, the arch of one eyebrow.

"I want you. This"—Connor knew Jed could feel his erection, just like he could feel Jed's too—"is for you. Not for the models or the art or anything but you. You turn me on so much."

Jed's head fell back and hit the door. "I w-wish I could talk all sw-sweet and f-f-filthy for you."

It came out like a confession. The sadness and yearning in Jed's voice tore at Connor. He let go of Jed's thigh and ran both hands up Jed's chest to clutch the sides of his face, and he kissed him again, soft plucking kisses, then deeper ones, then finally one that went on and on, taking the tension from Jed's shoulders and filling his lanky frame with a different tension, the tension of a man in lust. Connor loved that he could make Jed arch like this when they kissed slowly, squirm like that when Connor traced circles on his cheekbone with a thumb.

Jed put a hand up and pushed them apart. "D-d-dinner first."

Connor smiled. "I'm not much of a cook, but I'll help in the kitchen."

Jed led the way.

Dinner was salad and spaghetti with meatballs from the freezer warmed on the stove. After they sat down and Jed was pouring the wine, he confessed that his mother sometimes filled his freezer with his childhood favorites. Connor felt a pang for his own mother, who never had a chance to know her son as a grown-up, let alone cook his favorite foods for him.

"That's really nice."

Jed flinched, obviously seeing something in Connor's expression. "I j-just messed up, didn't I?"

Connor shook his head. "No. I just thought of my mom for a second. We're good."

"G-good." Jed grabbed Connor's hand and squeezed.

"Do you make your own dressing?" Connor held up the jar as he changed the subject. "From your crop?"

"Hannah m-makes it, but y-yes. From m-my crop."

"She should bottle it. It's very good."

"I'll t-tell her."

After dinner, Jed returned to the freezer and produced a small metal container, no larger than a pint, and a spoon.

"Ice cr-cream."

Some guys wax poetic about the perfect steak. Some guys search high and low for the perfect burger, or the best pizza in New York. Connor could appreciate those things, but when it came right down to it? Connor's favorite food indulgence had always been ice cream. Once, before she got sick, Connor's mom had taken him and Scott to Vermont for a weekend, and they'd visited the Ben & Jerry's factory. He'd been in little-boy heaven. It was one of the only family vacations they'd ever taken. For him, ice cream wasn't just food—it was his perfect comfort food.

"Only one spoon? Does that mean you're not going to share?"

Jed's smile was wicked. "Only need w-w-one."

He pulled the table away, then straddled Connor's lap. Gone was the shy lover needing reassurance. Setting the ice cream aside, Jed reached for the hem of Connor's shirt, lifting it up over his head, and then tossing it aside. Connor shuddered with sharp arousal—a bossy, toppy Jed was a hell of a turn-on.

Jed kissed Connor's bare chest, running a cold—damn it, ice cream!—hand through the chest hair. Icy fingers toyed with a nipple, and a hot erection ground into his own.

"Fuck, yeah." Connor tilted his head and groaned.

Picking up the ice cream and the spoon, Jed scooped some out and held it to Connor's lips. "H-homemade."

Connor opened his mouth. Blueberry, of course. It was sweet and tart together, and far creamier than any ice cream Connor had ever had from the store. He licked his lips and stared as Jed scooped up another spoonful and took his own bite.

Jed's lips closed around the spoon as if in slow motion, and he drew the spoon out of his mouth, then licked it, front and back. Connor had never wanted to be a spoon so bad in his life.

"M-more?" Jed teased, dipping the spoon into the ice cream again. Connor gripped the sides of the chair and nodded.

Jed trailed the cold spoon along Connor's collarbone, the sticky-sweet dessert cold and melty against his skin. Then, Connor got the same treatment the spoon had gotten, Jed's warm tongue licking the ice cream from his skin. He moaned, loving the contrast between the cold of the ice cream and the heat of Jed's tongue. The next spoonful went in his mouth, and damn, it tasted even better than the first, but Connor was starting to care less about dessert and more about the raging hard-on Jed's teasing had given him.

"C'mon, let's—"

Jed shook his head, taking another bite of ice cream. He rocked his hips a little, and the pressure on Connor's groin made him shake and bite his lip. "Fuck, Jed, please . . ."

Cold metal slid along the edge of Connor's ear, then Jed's tongue followed its path, ending with a nip at the lobe, hips still grinding, cold hands and lips teasing. Desire made Connor's limbs heavy, paralyzed by Jed's attentions and his own wantings.

"God, I want you to fuck me. Please."

Jed stilled on his lap, then stood up. "T-take off y-your pants. Lie on the fl-floor. I'll b-be right b-b-back."

And Jed thought he couldn't talk dirty.

That stammered order did more to rev Connor's motor than any raunchy monologue ever could. While Jed disappeared upstairs— *please let him be getting lube*—Connor stripped down, hesitating in his boxers.

For just a moment, he was the shy, fat kid again. The one who skipped prom not because he was gay, but because the tux rental place at the mall in Holyoke where all the other kids got their tuxes didn't carry his size.

For just a moment, he was afraid he wouldn't be wanted, and he started to lose his boner.

Then he saw his shirt on the floor and the ice cream on the table, and he lost the shorts instead. He stretched out on the floor next to the table, feeling silly and sticky, and still crazy aroused.

Jed came back and found him like that, arms behind his head, dick pointing in the air.

"Oh." That caught breath, that unguarded expression of wonder, did more for Connor's self-esteem than any diet had ever done for his waistline. He grabbed his cock, giving it a nice long stroke, and smiled up at Jed.

"See something you like?" He might be self-conscious about most of his body, but Connor had no shame in showing off his dick. Stroking with bigger, bolder movements than he would use alone in his bed, he didn't need to exaggerate the way it turned him on to have Jed watch him like this, waiting and wanting. He added a twist to his stroke and let his mouth drop open.

Jed was across the room and standing over him so fast, Connor had to laugh.

Dropping to his knees, Jed set the lube and a condom on the floor next to Connor. He ran two slender hands over Connor's chest, no longer ice-cream cold. He kneaded Connor's skin like a cat, and Connor arched off the floor, letting go of his dick and closing his eyes, letting the hard pressure of Jed's hands on his body alleviate any fears he had about being wanted.

"S-sexy." Jed pinched first one nipple, then the other, just hard enough to sting. "W-w-want to do so m-many things."

"Please, do them all." Connor opened his eyes and smiled. "And if we don't get to all of them tonight, we can try some tomorrow."

Jed's eyes were lust-dark, heavy-lidded, and his speech was slow, deliberate, and forceful. "Ton-night? W-we might not g-get to all of them in a l-li-lifetime."

And suddenly there was a lump in Connor's throat and tears stinging his eyes. He reached for Jed and pulled him down for a kiss, a long, leisurely, blueberry-ice cream-flavored kiss to hide the emotions that were tugging at him. Jed had words in his heart his lips could never say—every word was a minefield, a delicate navigation between self-expression and humiliation. And Jed had taken the time—and the words—to make Connor feel wanted, really fucking wanted.

Breathing hard, he broke the kiss. "How do you want me?"

Jed gestured for him to roll over, and Connor did, eagerly. Yeah, he'd love to see Jed's face, but it was good like this, on hands and knees while someone drove into him from behind. God, yes. He saw Jed's clothes join his in the pile on the floor, and he closed his eyes, taking slow, deep breaths as the anticipation built. Then Jed knelt behind him, tracing circles on his back with his palms.

One of those palms was cold.

Connor's eyes sprang open and he looked over his shoulder. Jed smiled at him, and the container of ice cream sat next to the lube on the floor. Wordlessly, Jed pulled out the spoon. The ice cream had melted some, though it wasn't liquid yet; it was still incredibly cold as Jed dropped a spoonful on his back, then used the spoon to drag it along his skin in a circle. Connor flinched, but then relaxed into the sensation as Jed dropped another spoonful, and another, and painted more shapes on Connor's skin.

When Jed licked each one from his body, it was all worth it. Jed's tongue—God, the man was talented with his tongue. He didn't just clean the ice cream off Connor's body, he wrote erotic love poetry in Connor's skin. The last icy drop rested right at the top of his crack, the base of his spine, and when he came to it, Jed traced concentric rings out until his tongue was dipping into the crease of Connor's ass and Connor widened his legs in invitation.

Jed bit one round ass cheek, then sat back, dropping the spoon in the ice cream container and picking up the lube.

"I've n-n-never done this."

Connor eyed Jed over his shoulder. "You've never topped?"

Jed laughed. "I've n-never . . ." He shrugged.

"Oh." Oh. It made sense that Jed's hookups might have been limited to hands and mouths. "Use lots of the lube. Go slow. I'll tell you if I don't like something."

Jed nodded. "O-okay."

For all his inexperience, Jed's hands were steady as he rubbed lube into Connor's rim, dipping a teasing finger inside. Connor's anticipation began to rise again, and he pushed into that finger. He glanced back, and the expression on Jed's face was heated and sharp as if this was something he'd never dared hope for. That look gave Connor the courage he needed to say the next bit.

"If you've really never done this before, and you wore condoms with the girls you've been with, I'm . . . I'm okay if you skip the condom."

The probing finger stilled, and Jed's mouth dropped open.

"Y-y-you?"

"I'm not New York's most eligible queer. It's been long enough since I've engaged in anything riskier than a blowjob that it would have shown up at my last physical."

Jed reached for the lube again, rubbing it over his bare cock. He groaned, and then leaned over Connor's back and kissed him, rough, sloppy, intense.

When Jed pressed his cock against Connor's entrance, Connor grabbed his own dick, keeping that hum of desire running through the initial resistance to the steady pressure of Jed opening him.

God, it felt good. Jed's strong hands held Connor's hips as he pushed inexorably inside. Knowing Jed was bare, that they were skin to skin—more intimate than Connor had been with anyone in years—it drove Connor crazy with desire. He shoved back harder, and Jed sank all the way in.

"Oh, oh, oh—" Jed gasped, and to Connor, it sounded like the sweetest praise.

"Fuck me, Jed, come on, harder," he begged. He wanted it rough enough to leave souvenirs on his skin. Wanted to remember all of this, being sticky with sweat and ice cream and stretched open, fucked by his beautiful farmer.

And Jed made him feel it.

Without dropping his hands from Connor's hips, he drove in. Each thrust brushed Connor's gland in a way that made his eyes water and his nipples tighten. No, Jed wasn't talking dirty, but he was making up for it by fucking Connor so hard and so good, Connor didn't ever want him to stop, even though orgasm was bearing down on him like a train in a tunnel.

He slid his hand faster along his dick, pressing his ass back toward Jed with each thrust, trying to memorize every second of this glorious fuck.

"I'm—I'm— Ahhhh, fuuuck."

Connor felt Jed's orgasm, felt the shudder and the wetness inside him, how everything went even more slick and the intensity of it was enough to propel him over the edge. He came, shaking and gasping Jed's name.

"So good. So g-good." Jed's hands rubbed Connor's back, his ass, his shoulders, his arms. "Gonna pull out."

Connor braced himself, missing the sensation of being filled as it slipped away. He flipped over and lay back on the floor, chuckling at the red lines of rug burn on his knees.

"I'm going to feel you for weeks," he laughed. "And I got cum and probably ice cream on your rug."

Jed flopped down beside Connor and kissed him like they'd never see each other again—somehow sated and hungry together.

"I d-d-don't care about the rug."

Connor smiled lazily, those delicious sex endorphins still crashing through him. "Are you always like that, all pushy and playful?"

Jed nipped at his ear. "Dunno. I'm like that w-with you."

"Let's grab a shower, and I'll help you with the dishes."

They shared the shower, kissing and cuddling under the spray of water. Jed's long, lanky body gleamed—suds and water highlighting his work-honed physique. Connor wanted to trace each line of muscle with his tongue and bite the firm swell of his ass. He settled for kissing the slender line of Jed's throat and reaching for the shampoo. As he tangled his hands in Jed's hair, Jed's brown eyes glowed like warm honey, and his hair stuck to his forehead and sent rivulets of soapy water along his chiseled cheekbones.

Jed could have been a model, easily. He had the body, and the face, and Connor knew he would be the perfect image of masculine beauty in a couture suit.

"I wish I could photograph you naked." He rubbed the washcloth across Jed's abs, then knelt and followed its path with his lips and tongue, the sweetness of the water contrasting with the salt of skin. Jed's cock made a valiant attempt to stiffen with Connor's lips so close, but then Jed tugged Connor to his feet.

"It'll pr-probably kill me to g-get hard ag-g-gain." He took the washcloth and circled it across the collarbone he had painted with ice cream. Then he carefully cleaned Connor's ear, turned him around, and scrubbed his back, ending with a teasing push of the cloth into the top of Connor's crack.

"Fuck." Connor leaned his forehead against the wall and pushed back.

"L-later," Jed murmured, wrapping his arms around Connor's waist. "I n-n-never had this before. It feels n-nice."

Connor rested his head on Jed's shoulder and smiled. "I'm glad I could give you your very first afterglow along with my ass."

Jed's body shook with laughter, and then Connor laughed too, and they were kissing and laughing with the water splashing all around them, and they didn't stop until it ran cold.

Chapter Nine

Connor's alarm went off at 4 a.m., and Jed flinched, pulling a pillow over his head. *Too early.* Sure, he still worked on Saturdays—plants didn't care about the calendar—but he usually started a little later.

"I'm so sorry," Connor whispered, his big body rolling away from Jed's as he attended to the alarm.

"Why are you w-whispering?"

"I don't know."

And then Connor's arms went around Jed, and his hands caressed Jed's chest, his cock rubbed Jed's ass, and Jed went boneless in that embrace. It felt so good, waking up like this. Too good, because it couldn't last. Connor would go home, and Jed would . . . Well, Jed would stay, because where else could he go? The farm, the town. This was home.

"Wish I could lie here with you all morning." Connor tweaked a nipple and bit at Jed's ear. "I'd blow you and then we could have breakfast and then you could fuck me again. I loved that. Wanna look in your eyes next time, see your face when you shoot."

Jed's breath caught at the intimacy of the memory. He'd never felt anything in his life quite like being inside Connor. When Connor's hand closed around his cock, the breath whooshed out of him on a groan.

"Yeah, just like that." Connor's hand slid along Jed's shaft, ramping him up. "You're so sexy like this. All sleepy-eyed."

"Con, I'm g-g-gonna—"

"Yeah." Connor sounded pleased—proud, even—as he stroked Jed faster, and Jed climbed up that peak, that point of no return when the ecstasy of the body overwhelmed everything he knew, and he shook in Connor's arms, coming hard and fast. When the shaking subsided, he realized Connor was still rubbing against his ass, kissing the back of his neck as he gentled him down. Eager to help Connor along, Jed clenched his cheeks to provide more friction. Connor moaned, so Jed humped back against him, loving the way Connor wasn't shy about rubbing off on him. It was dirty and sweaty and one hell of a way to greet the day.

A few more thrusts and Connor's own orgasm overtook him with a quiet grunt and a splash of sticky wet between them.

Jed rolled over and kissed Connor, not caring about morning breath, not after that orgasm. He loved the sensations of Connor's hands on his body, and of Connor's body under his own. They broke apart, gasping and laughing together.

"I'll make coffee," he offered, grateful for the post-sex lassitude that freed him, for a few moments at least, from his stutter.

"Thanks. I'll be quick in the shower." Connor gave Jed's shoulders one last sensual caress, then got out of bed and headed for the bathroom. Jed loved the way Connor moved, all sure of the world and his place in it. Just the sight of his broad, hair-covered chest had Jed wanting to go again, not to mention the sight of Connor's ass, all round and sexy in his boxer shorts. Jed pulled the pillow back over his face and groaned. What had he said to himself just yesterday about not getting attached? And then, "We might not get to all of them in a lifetime"? Making promises over pillow talk? He was setting himself up for heartbreak.

Jed hauled himself out of bed and went down to the kitchen. He started the pot of coffee—just Folgers, nothing fancy, and wondered if Connor would mind powdered cream.

He was digging the sugar out of the back of the cupboard when Connor came into the kitchen, rubbing at his wet hair with a towel.

Jed gestured to the mugs on the counter. "H-help your-s-self."

Connor studied the two mugs for a minute, and Jed blushed. One just had his name on it in brown letters. All capitals. The other was a travel mug from a bagel shop in Springfield. The rest of his mugs were in the dishwasher. When Connor picked up the "Jed" mug and filled it, Jed started a bit.

"Th-that's . . ."

Connor smiled. "I know. I get off a little on drinking from the cup with your name on it."

Jed blushed and passed him the sugar, watching Connor with greedy eyes as he measured out two spoonfuls.

"I d-don't have half-and-half." Jed offered the bottle of powdered cream he kept for when Hannah and Mike stayed over. Connor just shrugged.

"This works too. Thanks for the coffee. What do you say after I wrap today, we take a drive down to the reservoir?"

Jed frowned. So Connor didn't know about that either.

"R-r-road's closed."

"Closed? What do you mean?"

Jed nodded. "After n-nine eleven. No access."

Connor went still and his eyebrows shot up. "What do the high school kids do for fun then?"

Jed laughed. "S-same as always. G-get drunk and screw."

"I wish I'd known you back then." Connor cupped the side of Jed's face, ran a thumb along his cheekbone, and then dropped his hand. "I really do."

"W-w-would you have st-stayed?" Why had he asked that? He *knew* Connor wouldn't have stayed. But the fantasy of it took hold of him for a minute—that he could be enough. That someone would choose a simple life with him. But he saw the way Connor's face got tight and sad around the edges. Like he knew what it would mean to say yes, but also like he cared too much to lie.

Connor swallowed. "I'd have carried you away with me."

But that was an even more dangerous fantasy. What was there for Jed outside of this?

He flushed, started to say he was just kidding, but all that came out was the word "I" and a string of consonants.

"Hey." Connor pulled him into a hug. "Let's just think of something else to do."

What Jed wanted was to close the front door of the farmhouse against the rest of the world, to take Connor to bed, and to learn every inch of his body. To take his greedy fill of intimacy and mutual attraction and how good it felt to seduce and be seduced. But he also understood Connor's need to be out in the world.

"Wh-whatever you w-want." He walked to the coffeemaker, poured his own cup, and came back to wrap an arm around Connor's waist, pulling him in for a kiss on the temple. "We could g-g-go to dinner?"

Connor looked surprised, then kissed Jed. "Burger King?" he teased as he pulled away.

"We could g-g-go somewhere in W-Westfield."

Connor nodded. "Yeah, that would be nice. You don't mind being seen in public with a known homosexual?"

"Of course not. You're my fr-friend." A wicked grin spread across Jed's face. "Ish."

"Nothing 'ish' about it." Connor leaned in for another kiss.

That kiss over coffee was the highlight of Jed's day. While he was doing his morning check of the grounds, he found another group of bushes with shoestring, and they weren't in the field adjacent to the Rancocas. Though the season was almost over and the crop was nearly in, if some of the remaining late-producers didn't turn out a healthy yield, it could hurt his end-of-year income drastically.

Fucking bugs.

He kicked at the ground. If he wanted to keep his organic certification, he couldn't treat the plants with pesticides. His crop was worth more certified. But if the aphids spread the disease to other fields, he'd lose even more of his crop.

And, it being Saturday, he was all alone dealing with the task—tagging the diseased bushes, checking row by row for any symptoms. By lunchtime, he'd marked seven bushes, and his mood was black—not even the text he got from Connor could cheer him up.

Hey, I'm sending Candace out to Burger King to fetch us some lunch, want a Whopper? xo, C

Jed frowned at the message, irritated by the interruption, annoyed with himself for being irritated. Finally, he typed back. *No, thanks.*

I'm having a major problem in the east field, needs all my attention right now. I'll text you when I'm ready to pack it in.

When his phone beeped a moment later, he growled in frustration.

You need to eat—come on, let me buy my guy a burger. Please?

Jed didn't even think before he typed his answer. *I don't need a keeper, Connor. And I'm not "your guy." I have work to do.*

Connor didn't text again.

Jed kept working, sweating, cursing. There were too many plants for him to dig them all up and burn them himself. He called Mike, ready to stutter out a plea for help, only to discover that Mike and Hannah had left Billy with Mom and taken a weekend getaway, just the two of them.

Which only made Jed angrier. This was the weekend he was supposed to be spending with Connor. Sure, Connor was working, and he was working too, but it wasn't supposed to go like this. They were supposed to have a little time together— *Ah, shit.*

Jed pulled out his phone.

I'm so sorry.

He didn't get an answer right away—and he didn't expect one since Connor was shooting photos in his north fields, but he knew he'd feel uneasy until he had a chance to make it right.

When he heard the car engine behind him, he turned around to see Connor stepping from the rental car, paper Burger King bag in hand. Silently, he held it out to Jed.

"I'm—s-s-s-s—" Jed tried—he took a deep breath and tried again, and a third time, and finally Connor took pity on him.

"Shhhh." He walked up to Jed and put an arm around his waist, pulling him into a hug. "I'm not mad. You were right. I don't have any claim on you, and I was being pushy. Yeah, your words stung, but they're just words. And I got you the burger anyway. Here."

Jed stepped back and took the bag. "W-w-words are pr-p-precious."

Connor nodded. "So let's not waste them hurting each other. What's going on out here? You said it was a major problem."

Jed broke a branch off the nearest infected bush and held it up for Connor to see. The stems were the wrong color, and the fruit had ripened to a dull red instead of a deep blue.

"Sh-sh-shoestring. Insect-spread disease. A d-dozen bushes."

Connor whistled. "How do you treat it?"

"Y-y-you don't. You d-dig. You b-burn."

"Ah, hell, Jed, I'm sorry. I had no idea."

Jed shrugged. "How's the sh-shoo-shoot?"

Connor smiled. "We're taking a few hours off for lunch and to let the light change. Can I help you out here?"

"Y-you c-can talk to me w-w-while . . ." He held up his burger. Leaning against the car, he unwrapped it. Connor came and leaned next to him.

"I can do that. I happen to be excellent lunchtime company. So, it turns out Sebby's boyfriend called while they were at the club last night, and it turned into big drama-rama—Seb saying he would bend over the bar and let every guy in the place fuck him if John didn't agree to something, and Oliver and Henry ended up hauling Seb out of there before he could do it. That kid looks pretty for the camera, but he is *insane*."

Jed didn't follow the names, but he didn't really think he needed to. He got the point. He nodded and took another bite of his burger, gesturing for Connor to keep talking.

"Anyway, staying in was the right choice. They all showed up this morning hungover and grumpy, and Seb has spent every minute he's not in front of the camera leaving desperate apology voice mails for his Johnnie."

Jed shook his head. He understood gossip—he lived in a small town, there was always gossip.

"Strange f-folk."

Connor laughed. "Yeah. So, that's been my morning. And yours has been disease and mayhem in the blueberry bushes. So, I'd call it even. Where'd you learn about farming?"

"I g-gardened—a lot. Then in c-college," Jed managed between bites of the burger. "Studied sus-sustainable ag-agriculture. Organic f-farming. Lots of chemistry. D-did you know there are farms on r-rooftops in New Y-York?"

"That's really cool." Connor smiled at him. "God, I want to ask you all kinds of questions, 'cause I'm dying to know everything about you, but don't want to put you on the spot to answer."

Jed laughed, trying not to let the bitterness overwhelm him. "I'm—I'm trapped. M-m-my stutter. I w-want to tell y-you everything. Maybe I'll wr-write you a letter."

"You have my email address." Connor grinned. "Forgive me for prying but, did you ever have speech therapy?"

"S-s-some. It d-d-didn't help m-much. Started too l-late."

"And you just stopped?"

Jed glared at Connor. "It w-w-wasn't my ch-choice." If it had been, how would things be different? He'd have gone to public school, gotten speech therapy when he was young enough to do him any good, but how was he supposed to know when he was a child that what his parents thought—no, believed, because it was a question of faith for them—was the right thing would lead to his loneliness and isolation? By the time they all understood he wouldn't "outgrow" the stutter, his parents were committed to homeschooling him and his younger brothers. When there was time and money enough, he went to therapy—but it wasn't the same as what a public school would have provided.

He'd trusted them, as children do. And now he was thirty-five years old and barely able to express himself. It made him angry, so angry, though he still didn't doubt his parents had made their choices out of love and fear for him.

"Sorry, that was none of my business."

"They d-didn't know any better," Jed offered as explanation. It was all he had, and it appeared to be as cold a comfort to Connor as it had been to him.

"I don't understand. I don't know how they couldn't want more for you . . ."

Jed bristled. "M-more than w-w-what? Farming?"

"No!" Connor shook his head. "No, of course that's not what I meant. I mean . . . I see how it hurts you to not be able to say everything you want to. To have to fight for every word. And I don't understand how parents could just . . . just take it on faith."

Connor was clearly walking on eggshells now, trying to be diplomatic.

"It d-d-doesn't matter."

"It should matter. What did praying about it ever fix?"

Jed's face grew hot. "F-faith isn't always about f-fixing."

"So, what is it about?"

How was he supposed to explain something as huge as faith? "H-hope, I guess. Tr-trust. My parents aren't p-perfect. But they love me."

Connor dropped his gaze. "I'm sorry. I'm sure they love you. I didn't mean to suggest—"

"W-w-would you like to meet them?" Jed found himself asking after swallowing the last bite of his burger.

"Oh, here." Connor reached through the car window and pulled out a soda. "Got this for you too. I'd love to meet your family. You know I'm driving home Monday though."

"Come to ch-church." Jed smiled. "Your brother g-goes."

Connor shuddered dramatically, and Jed saw the exact moment that Connor realized he was serious.

"You're not joking, are you? Me? In church?"

Jed studied the crumpled ball of paper in his hand.

"And br-brunch after."

Connor ran a hand through his hair and gave Jed another one of those "Am I being punked?" stares. Finally, he tossed his hands up in the air. "Fine, but if the whole place goes up in flames when I walk through the door tomorrow, it's on you."

Jed smiled. "Y-you a bad man?"

Connor licked his lips, and the sight went straight to Jed's groin. "An unrepentant sinner, I'm afraid."

"W-we all sin, Connor."

Connor scrubbed a hand across his face. "Yeah, but you feel bad about it afterward."

Jed grabbed that hand and brought it to his lips, dropping a quick kiss on Connor's knuckles. "W-w-won't ever reg-g-gret you. Nev-never."

Chapter Ten

Oh, god, this is a terrible idea.

When they entered the church, Connor was torn between grabbing Jed's hand and bolting for the door. Nerves like this were rare for him, usually only brought on by acute stage fright. He hadn't been in church for anything other than weddings or funerals since he'd announced to his mother at the age of thirteen that he was done going. She'd invited him a few more times, but he'd always gotten out of it. Apparently, Jed was more persuasive than Connor's mother.

He balled his hands into fists at his side, trying not to notice the stares as he followed Jed to the pew where his family sat. Kind of in the middle, not too close. Connor would have preferred the back row, but it wasn't like he had a choice, right? He glanced around, but didn't see Scott. Was it so wrong to hope that Scott's attendance wasn't as steadfast as Jed's?

He was surprised when Jed's brother Mike stood up to introduce him to the rest of the family. "Hi, Connor, hi, Jedidiah. Mom, Dad this is Connor Graham, he's staying at the farm with Jed for the weekend. Connor, the surly-looking guy on the end is our brother David, and Luke is behind him with his wife, Torrie."

The brothers and Torrie all smiled and murmured a welcome. Jed's dad stuck out his hand for a shake, and Jed's mom, after handing a wriggling Billy over to Hannah, did the same.

"You're Bruce Graham's boy?" she asked.

"Nephew, actually. Bruce was my mom's brother."

The whole family murmured a rush of condolences, and Connor nodded his thanks.

"S-sit here." Jed gestured to the end of the pew behind his family. "L-Luke and Torrie m-made r-r-room."

Connor sat, beads of sweat forming on his brow. He grabbed his pocket square and tried to dab at them surreptitiously, but he felt like the eyes of the entire congregation were upon him.

At the beginning of the service, everyone stood and greeted the people around them, and several welcomed him to their church. He gave each an awkward nod and then sat down when everyone else did. Okay, so far, not so bad.

When the sermon started, he tried to pay attention. He really did. But when he peeked over at Jed, who followed along with the reading in his Bible, lips moving silently, a finger tracing well-worn pages, his breath caught.

The day before, he'd laughed off his discomfort with church, only agreeing to attend for Jed's sake. Though he'd still never call himself a Christian, watching Jed as he listened to the sermon was something akin to a religious experience—his obvious joy was moving. Connor would likely never be a believer himself, but he liked seeing Jed's face light up like this. When everyone rose to sing, Jed shared his hymnal with Connor. Connor didn't know the tune, but he sang along gamely, trying to match pitch with Jed's singing—not a stutter to be heard. Jed had a rich tenor, and he smiled as he sang. Connor was utterly, completely captivated.

After the service, Scott approached him in the parking lot.

"What are you doing here?"

"I was invited."

Scott's face turned sour. "I saw you sitting with Jed Jones. Are you trying to fuck things up for me? Trying to hold on to the farm?"

"I don't think you're allowed to say 'fuck' in church, Scott."

"What would you know about it, it's not like you ever went. What are you even doing in town? Don't you have a life and a job in the city?"

"Don't you have one here?" Connor hissed. "I held a photo shoot at the farm and stayed at the big house. Jed invited me to church. We're friends, have you got a problem with that?"

Jed appeared at his side, giving Scott a cool once-over. "G-Graham."

"Jedidiah, if you'll excuse—"

"His name is Jed. Only his family calls him Jedidiah," Connor interrupted, irritated by his brother's attempts to control everything. "And if you're just coming over here to berate me for my life choices, or for being a big gay city-boy, then don't bother. I've heard it all before from better men than you."

He turned on his heel to find Jed's whole family standing behind him.

Oh yeah, he would be that guy. First time in church and he got into a fight in the parking lot.

At least it hadn't come to blows.

Jed gave Connor a loaded look. "Let's g-go have brunch."

"Yeah. Let's do that."

They drove out past the ski area, and, from the passenger seat, Connor watched the scenery pass in mute curiosity, struck by how a place could be so foreign and so familiar at the same time. How many times had he skied—right *there*—as a child? But the summer sun made the mountain curves look entirely different. He used the silence to try to piece together some kind of explanation for the fight with Scott, but his whole life he'd felt bewildered by Scott's hostility, and he couldn't find the words.

"I hope I didn't embarrass you," he said finally.

Jed smiled across the cab at him. "There'll be g-goss-gossip at the table for sure."

Connor knuckled his eyes and winced. "Ugh. I'm so sorry. I don't get him. I don't understand why he's always such a dick to me. Why he assumes I'm trying to fuck something up for him. He knows I want to put this all behind us as soon as possible, but he's mean and suspicious and I don't know why."

Jed's face had gone drawn and hurt looking. "P-p-put all this b-b-be-behind you?"

Ah, shit.

"That's not— Goddamn it Jed."

Jed flinched.

Fuck. The profanity thing. "I'm sorry, I did it again. And after church and everything. I am messing this up so hard. I didn't mean you. I meant—the farm."

"The f-f-farm I r-rent."

Connor couldn't help it. He got mad. The farm was always going to be between them, and it sucked. It was also the thing bringing them together, and without it, what excuse would Connor have for even seeing Jed? It would be over. And that's not what Connor wanted.

"Do you ever think you might want more than that?"

"M-more than w-what?"

Connor gestured out the window. "This tiny town which has not changed—no, I'm sorry, they've closed some roads, and the elementary school, and they turned off the stoplight, but aside from that, *has not changed*—since we were children."

"My f-family is here."

"So is mine," Connor pointed out.

"Your br-brother is not like m-mine."

"Wouldn't *they* want more for you?"

He could see the muscle twitching in Jed's jaw, could see the strain of Jed holding back, always in control. He wanted Jed to lose that control.

"*They* w-want me close."

"You deserve more."

"I l-like farming. It makes me happy."

"I don't want this to be over," Connor whispered.

"You c-can't always have your w-way. My choices are imp-p-portant too." Jed shook his head and pulled the truck to the side of the road where a row of cars sat empty like a parking lot. "R-road's w-washed out ahead." He opened his door and hopped down, then stood waiting for Connor.

Connor walked around the truck. Instead of asking Jed which direction, he pushed him back against the truck and kissed him. Not a long, drawn-out thing, just a quick, hard kiss on the lips.

"Our situation? It sucks. But the time I spend with you is precious to me. Let's not spend it fighting."

Jed peered around furtively before kissing Connor back just as quickly. Then he shoved Connor away and started walking.

There was nothing Connor could do but follow.

The house, which was tucked back from the dirt road and up a hill, was shockingly tiny. And Connor was a New Yorker—he knew tiny.

Jed's family was big—four sons.

"Is this . . . is this where you grew up?" he asked.

Jed glanced over his shoulder at Connor and nodded.

Connor had grown up without a lot of money. He remembered his mom bitching when the child support payments came late—or didn't come at all. His mom had been a lifelong renter of places that never seemed big enough, and Bruce may have been land-rich, but he'd often been cash-poor.

But it had just been Connor and his mom and Scott until Scott went to college, then Connor and his mom until they moved in with Bruce. Even the small apartments they'd rented seemed like luxury compared to the house in front of Connor.

"And your parents had four boys?"

Jed laughed. "Yeah, I had to sh-share a bedroom with all of them. Sch-sch-school at the kitchen table." He shook his head. "Seems cr-criminal to have the f-f-farmhouse to mys-self."

Connor held his tongue. He wasn't a snob, and he could see how growing up in tight quarters had made for the close relationships Jed and his brothers shared as adults. But he didn't think for a second that Jed should feel bad about having privacy for the first time in his life.

A Bible verse, faded to unreadable by the sunlight, graced the welcome mat, and dried flowers and pinecones were worked into a wreath hung on the door, which Jed opened without knocking. The kitchen was full of people. The brothers and Jed's dad were seated at the table with a plate of donuts, while the wives and Jed's mom were cooking and chopping.

Everyone was bustling around and talking over each other, but they all stopped when Jed and Connor walked in.

One of Jed's brothers—Luke?—cleared his throat, and Jed's mom flapped her hands at them and told Jed's dad to take the donuts—and their guest—and go sit in the living room.

Connor hoped the disbelief didn't show on his face as the men all stood and walked out of the room while the women kept working. It was like something out of an old TV show. And Jed didn't seem to think anything was strange about it?

As Jed and Connor sat down on a worn-looking sofa, Billy came careening out of a hallway in nothing but a diaper, followed by a harried-looking Hannah.

"Nap time, Billy. Now." She held up his clothing. "I don't care if you sleep naked, but you need to go get in bed."

The toddler started crying, and launched himself at Jed, who scooped him up and tickled him.

"I'll t-take him," he told Hannah once Billy was smiling again. He stood and carried the little boy out of the room.

Hannah collapsed on the couch next to Connor and buried her face in his shoulder. "I just need a minute, thanks," she mumbled onto his sleeve.

He laughed. That unself-conscious snuggle was the most normal thing that had happened since he walked into the house, and he liked the easy affection from Jed's sister-in-law. She straightened up and smiled at him.

"That kid is impossible sometimes. Uncle Jed seems to be the only one who can get through to him. He is totally the baby whisperer. So, how'd you like church?"

Connor winced. "It was nice?"

She didn't seem offended. "I don't think the sermon was as clear as it could have been, but it was better than last week's."

"Jed seemed pretty into it."

Across the room, Mike chuckled. "Jed's always so serious in church. Like there's gonna be a test on it."

"Well, there is, Mikey. It's called 'life,'" Luke piped up. "Nothing wrong with paying attention."

"And see, that right there—" Hannah pointed at Luke "—is more honest-to-god theology than we've heard in church in the last six months. I'm telling you, Pastor Green is not a deep thinker."

Connor was fascinated. It never occurred to him that Jed's churchgoing family might have discussion and debate over what they heard there. It made him wish he had paid better attention to the sermon. But when he racked his brain, all he remembered was Jed's mouth open, brown eyes sparkling, rich tenor voice set free in song.

"Jed doesn't stutter when he sings," Connor said.

"Never has," Luke said. "Always confused the heck out of me how he could sing and read out loud, and yet, his own words—"

"G-get stuck," Jed finished from the doorway.

Luke shrugged, half apology, half "what can you do?"

Hannah stood. "Gonna go see if Mom needs help in the kitchen." Jed came and took her place.

"Is it always like that? The women working in the kitchen like a fifties sitcom?" Connor whispered.

Shaking his head and smiling, Jed whispered back, "They w-want to g-gossip about you." He scanned the room, and his jaw stiffened. Connor followed his gaze.

Jed's dad sat in a recliner, eating a donut. Mike sat in the other chair, and the other two brothers were standing. While Connor and Jed sat alone on a couch big enough for all four of them.

Connor flushed.

"W-why don't you g-g-guys sit down," Jed ground out.

Luke glanced at Connor, and then at his feet. Hannah had cuddled right up to Connor, but the brothers were—not afraid of him, not exactly, but uncomfortable.

"Maybe they think queerness is catching."

Luke blushed and Mike laughed, but the laugh was stiff and awkward. Next to Connor, Jed stiffened and fisted his hand at his side.

"If it was, wouldn't Jed be gay by now?" David joked.

Oh shit. Connor saw the anger ripple across Jed's face, and he set what he hoped was a calming hand on Jed's knee.

"Jed, don't."

Jed stared down at that hand, that too-intimate-for-just-friends touch, and the rest of the men looked at it too. Connor jerked his hand away, regretting giving in to his impulses—first to speak, then to touch.

"And i-i-i-if . . ." Jed took a breath. "I-i-if I am? Is th-th-that a pr-prob-prob—"

"Aw, man." Luke made a disgusted face. "That isn't funny, Jed."

"I'm n-n-not jok-joking."

The room erupted in noise, all of the brothers talking at once, and Jed just glared at them. Hannah and Torrie came in from the kitchen to see what the fuss was about, and when they realized, they both stared at Jed and Connor.

Jed picked up Connor's hand and held it tightly in his own, and Connor squeezed it as they waited for the noise to die down. His heart ached for Jed. Sure, he'd follow Jed's lead, but really he wanted nothing more than to wrap Jed in his arms, carry him away, and soothe his hurt.

"—and what about Jennifer Parker?" Mike shouted and everyone finally stopped talking and faced Jed.

"W-w-what about her?" Jed said softly.

"We thought you and her were getting serious," Torrie said.

"Y-you could have as-asked."

"Jed," Connor whispered, "you don't have to explain yourself."

Jed patted his hand. "N-no. But I'm d-done lying."

"I don't think this—any of this—is appropriate conversation for Sunday brunch." Jed's dad got to his feet. "Jed, apologize to your brothers."

Jed blanched and rocked back in his seat.

"Excuse me?" Connor stood. "Mr. Jones? Why should he apologize?"

"Yeah, Dad, why should Jed apologize?" Hannah asked, surprising Connor. At least Jed had one family member at his back.

"He brought this all in the house, he needs to clean it up," Jed's father answered and, with that, walked out of the room.

Jed's brothers started arguing again, talking over each other and cutting each other off, but Connor had heard enough. He turned to Jed, whose eyes had gone wide and breath shallow.

"You wanna get out of here?" he asked.

Jed nodded.

When Connor spoke next, it was to Hannah. "Give your mother-in-law my apologies, but there are going to be two fewer seats at the table. I'm taking him home now."

Hannah nodded, glancing at her husband, who was still arguing with his brothers, all of them ignoring both Jed and Connor.

Connor guided Jed out the back door instead of through the kitchen, and then around the house and down to the muddy dirt road. He was still holding Jed's hand: it might be epically stupid if one of Jed's brothers decided he wasn't okay with this and came after them, but Connor needed that touch, and more than that, Jed needed it too.

Jed's face was white, his eyes wide, and he was shaking, with fear, anger, or shock, Connor couldn't tell. He steered Jed around the big sinkhole where the road had washed out, and then the cars were there, glittering in the sunlight.

"Keys." Jed slapped them into his outstretched hand and Connor unlocked the truck and opened the door. Once Jed was settled into the passenger seat, Connor got behind the wheel and started driving. "Are you okay?"

Jed shook his head.

"Okay, here's what we're going to do. I'm going to take you home, and we're going to get our laptops, and we're going to open a chat window, and we'll talk. We'll talk as long and as much as you need to. You can—"

"Connor," Jed stopped him. "I d-don't need th-that."

Connor swallowed. Okay. They could talk-talk. That worked too. "Okay. Okay, we can just regular talk. I'm sorry. I thought it might be easier for you. Sorry. I shouldn't have."

"Connor," Jed repeated, more forcefully. "W-what I n-n-need is you to t-take me home, and m-m-make it not hurt."

God, Jed was killing him here. Connor took a deep, shaky breath. "I don't know if I can make it not hurt, honey. I want to, but that was hurtful shit."

Jed laughed, a hollow little laugh, and glared out the window before turning back to Connor. "Then m-m-make me f-f-forget."

That Connor could do.

Later, he wouldn't remember parking the truck, and god only knows how he got Jed in the house and upstairs to bed.

He wouldn't remember where their clothes dropped or how he slipped on the second stair from the top and almost fell.

But he'd never forget the rough texture of Jed's hands carding through the hair on his chest, or the heat of his lips, kissing in quiet, lonely desperation.

He'd never forget the way Jed arched and groaned when Connor took him in his mouth. He'd never forget Jed's choked-off sob when he came, the taste of him on his tongue, or the way Jed took him in hand afterward and made him shake and shout.

More than anything, he'd never forget how when Jed cried, he turned his face into Connor's chest and held on like Connor was his anchor. That he could be strong for Jed in a way no one had been for him when he'd come out, it meant something.

The next morning, their kisses held a sharper, poignant edge. They fucked quietly but frantically in the predawn darkness, as if they could say all they needed to with their bodies alone. Connor did everything he could to make Jed feel good, to make him feel wanted and worthy; all the ways a person should feel in the arms of a lover.

And then Jed made him breakfast, and they ate in near-silence. Jed read the comics from the Sunday *Republican*, and Connor Facebooked. Finally though, he spoke.

"Jed. We gotta talk about it."

Setting the paper aside, Jed turned all his attention to Connor. "About w-what?"

"Me leaving. Going home. No more photo shoot or plans to come back. Is this how it ends? I mean—I don't have any idea what you want."

Jed didn't meet his eyes. "What I w-w-want isn't imp-p-portant."

"It's important to me."

Jed picked up his phone and started typing, fingers flying across the screen. After a moment, Connor's beeped.

I want to grow things, with a man at my side. I want to hold my head high in church and live my life without lying or hurting people. And I want to see more of the world than the little corner of it willing to wait patiently for me to talk. I want you. I want you so much, I shake with it. When you drive away, it's going to hurt so bad, so I don't want to talk about what I want. I just want to pretend it isn't ending.

Connor's breath rushed out. "Jed, I—"

Jed was watching him, eyes glittering and knuckles turning white around his phone. It was impossible. This was Jed's home, in a way it had never been his. They couldn't do this indefinitely without someone getting hurt. But . . . was there any reason it had to end now?

"I'm only two hours away. We can see each other sometimes. You could come see me in New York. I would really like that."

Jed started typing again.

We can text.

Connor nodded. "Yeah."

We can sext.

They both laughed.

Jed stared at him for what seemed like an eternity, then texted one more time.

I'll come after the harvest.

Connor smiled. "See, it's not ending." And then he got up and started doing the dishes, and Jed came and joined him. They kissed and cuddled as they worked, until Connor set the frying pan in the drying rack, pulled Jed to him with soapy hands, and whispered, "One more time."

But as he drove away that morning with the sun rising at his back, he was raw and inside out and alone. The slender figure on the front porch grew smaller in his rearview mirror, and it felt like an ending.

Jed watched Connor drive away, and then crossed the driveway to the trailer and went inside.

Hannah gazed up at him with big, guilty-looking eyes.

"I sent the crews out," she said. "I thought you might be a little late coming in."

"How l-l-long have you kn-known?" He sat down heavily in the chair.

"I didn't!" She straightened and the surprise on her face seemed genuine. "I just didn't like the way they all were talking at you and around you and your dad saying you should apologize. Ugh." She stuck out her tongue. "They're the ones who should be apologizing to you. Anyway. Mike is coming by to help you with the plants you found with shoestring. I arranged the burn permit too."

Jed cringed. Was he ready to face his brother? He'd always valued Mike's approval most. As far back as he could remember, he'd followed Mike like an eager puppy, idolizing him—even trusting Mike to speak on his behalf. Mike's disapproval would be a deeper cut than he was ready to risk.

But ready or not, it looked like this conversation was going to happen. And he had Hannah at his back. That wasn't nothing.

"Th-thank you." Jed's heart thumped wildly as he stood. "Hiring you w-was the best id-idea."

"You look like you need a hug." She didn't wait for an answer, just stood up, came around the desk, and gave him one. "You're okay, Jedidiah. The family will be okay. Have faith."

"I w-w-want to." He squeezed her once, then let go.

"Mike will be here in an hour. I've got paperwork to do and calls to make, so why don't you stop by the barn and make sure the CSA boxes are ready to go out this afternoon?"

Jed nodded and took her advice.

When Mike arrived and grunted a "hello," Jed gestured toward the truck and they headed straight for the east field, neither saying a word until they started digging. Jed was used to silence with his brother—but silence because you didn't have anything to say felt different than silence brought on by fear.

Jed hacked a little more violently at a stubborn root.

"Jedidiah, I'm sorry."

Jed stopped digging and faced his brother. "W-w-we gonna do this n-now?"

"You can just listen." Mike gave him a nervous smile. "I love you, you know that, right? And before you go thinking Hannah put me up to this, she and I talked about you a lot yesterday, and we prayed for you—"

Jed scoffed and shook his head and dug his shovel into the dirt.

"—we prayed for you, not because we wanted to make you un-gay or anything. We prayed that the world would be kind to you and that no one would hurt you, and we knew, the way you do, that sometimes you have to be the first person to do the thing you're praying for."

Jed turned his gaze back to Mike and wiped sweat from his eyes. "Y-you decided n-not to hurt me."

Mike shuffled his feet and wouldn't meet Jed's eyes. "My reaction yesterday was hurtful. I'm sorry, and I hope you'll forgive me. It's really important that you know I'm not ashamed of you or afraid of you. What I *am* is very much afraid for you. That someone will beat you up or hurt you, because I watch the news, Jed, I see these headlines, and I don't want that for you."

Jed swallowed, relief washing over him. He and Mike were okay. "I'm c-careful."

"The rest of them will come around. I promise. Even Dad."

"H-h-hope so." Jed flinched.

"They didn't raise us to hate." Mike started digging once more. "You know that."

Jed nodded.

"So, Connor Graham, huh?" There was a teasing note to Mike's voice now.

A slow smile worked its way across Jed's face. He thought about Connor, so earnest in his belief that they could keep seeing each other, even though it was completely crazy, and Jed's heart sped up. Maybe the kind of relationship he wanted, the kind he craved, was impossible with Connor in New York. But the fantasy still made him go all soft inside.

"He's . . . he's so *n-n-nice*, Mike."

Mike rubbed his shirt across his face and smiled. "You don't say that the way you used to say that Jennifer was nice."

Jed's own laughter at that surprised him. "He's nice in a d-different w-way."

Mike was right, they hadn't been raised to hate. But nothing Jed had been taught about love had prepared him for Connor.

The next time Jed saw the rest of his family was the following Sunday at church. He was running late, and the church was already full when he arrived. Luke's back stiffened a little when he saw Jed, but he waved and gestured for Jed to sit with him and Torrie. David didn't meet his eyes. Disgusted? Or embarrassed? Jed wasn't good at reading his youngest brother. In the row in front of them, Jed's mother offered him a faltering smile, but then Pastor Green started speaking, and she faced forward again.

The sermon stretched interminably, with the pastor droning on and following tangent after tangent like he'd never heard of rehearsing these things. Jed tuned him out, taking the opportunity to peer around the congregation.

Here and there, a gaze skittered away from his, and he flushed. Had the gossip mill started spinning so quickly? He focused his attention back on the minister.

"... I will be replaced by Reverend Brenda Hopkins, who will be relocating here at the end of next month."

Wait, what? Jed turned to Luke and Torrie, who shrugged.

"First I've heard he was leaving," she whispered.

"Good riddance," Luke muttered.

Jed tried to catch Dad's attention after, but the man made a beeline for his Buick, and Jed's mom followed. His stomach sank.

"You coming to brunch?" Hannah bumped his arm. Billy held her hand and swung it between them, giggling.

"Y-you think they w-want me there?"

She sighed. "Of course they want you there."

But watching the Buick pull away, Jed didn't share her confidence. "I n-need to change the oil in the tr-truck. Have an ex-extra donut for me."

In the weeks after Connor returned to the city, he worked relentlessly and lived for the texts from Jed. Yeah, sure, some of them were sexy. Raunchy, explicit descriptions of how exactly Jed would fuck him the next time they were together. Soon Connor practically sprung wood every time his phone beeped. But most of the texts were photos—moments from Jed's life. Moments that made Connor feel like part of that life.

The last of the crop is in. Getting the farm ready for winter.

Accompanied by a picture of empty carriers stacked in the barn. Connor texted back that he was impressed by Jed's eye for composition, which started a long discussion about photography and the rule of thirds and how Jed could use different apps on his phone to caption his photos.

Took Billy to the fair this weekend. Hannah's salad dressing—the one you liked so much—took first place. Miss you like crazy.

A selfie of Jed and Billy with cotton candy and matching blue-stained tongues.

We're getting a new minister at church. Rumor has it she's a lesbian with a really pretty wife.

That one made Connor's eyebrows raise, but then he smiled. A lesbian minister in the big white church could be a good thing. He wondered how the theology discussions at Jed's family brunches would go. He'd asked a few times about how Jed's family was treating him, but only received back a terse *They're okay.*

But the text he'd been waiting for, the one he'd hoped for since August, the one he refused to ask for, because it needed to come from Jed, came on Halloween night as he walked home from the bodega with bags of sweets for trick-or-treaters.

What are you doing for thanksgiving? Thought i might come to new york. if you'd be around.

His hands shook as he texted back.

Having dinner with you.

After a long moment, the reply came.

I hoped you'd say that.

If Connor punched the air and shouted, startling a pigeon, he still wasn't the weirdest person in Brooklyn by a mile.

Chapter
Eleven

The new minister was not, in fact, a lesbian with a real pretty wife. Well, she might've been a lesbian, but she hadn't said, so Jed wasn't about to ask. But she definitely wasn't married. Standing outside her office, he wiped his palms on his jeans. Was he crazy for coming here for counseling of all things? Didn't that involve lots of talking? But she'd responded to his email so quickly, suggesting this initial session, that he'd agreed without thinking.

The big white church had been built as a gathering place, a community house, simple in architecture and ornamentation. The new pastor had taken her cue from the rest of the building and left the door to the minister's office unadorned except for her name. *Rev. Brenda Hopkins.* When Jed knocked, the echo filled the hallway.

"Come in!"

He pushed the door open and took his first up-close-and-personal look at Pastor Hopkins. She was young—maybe younger than him—with a blond ponytail and brown eyes. Her smile was wide and genuine, and her jeans and T-shirt obviously well loved. Boxes stood stacked by the desk, and two Bibles lay open, pages down, on the desk. He liked her immediately.

"Hi. I'm Jed J-Jones." He stuck out his hand.

"Mr. Jones, it's so nice to meet you." She shook it. "I'm sorry the place is a disaster, I'm still moving in, but your email intrigued me, and I wanted to meet you right away." She talked a mile a minute, waving her hands for emphasis. "Go ahead and have a seat. Do you want a cup of coffee?"

Jed shuddered involuntarily. He'd had the church coffee enough times in his life to know only the very faithful or very desperate would touch it. "No, th-thank you."

She laughed. "It's not the same stuff we brew for meetings. I brought my Keurig. Even we ministers have our vices."

"In th-that case, I w-would love a cup. Black, please." He smiled, some of the tension leaving his shoulders.

She gestured toward the chair again, and then bustled through the doorway. When she returned, two steaming mugs in hand, he started to stand, but she shook her head so he stayed put.

She set the coffee down on a thick printout sitting on the desk. "Don't worry about spills. It's just paper."

He smiled and took the cup. "Thank you, P-Pastor Hopkins."

"Brenda, please."

"Pastor Br-Brenda."

"So, you said in your message you're having something of a crisis of faith? Let's talk about that."

He took a sip of the coffee. This would be his first time saying the words to a near-stranger, and it gave him an exhilarating thrill. It terrified him and gave him strength at the same time. He lifted his chin and spoke slowly.

"I'm gay."

She sat up straighter. "Okay. Is that common knowledge in the congregation? I don't want to assume and accidently out you."

That's it?

Trying—and probably failing—to mimic her nonchalance, he shrugged and searched for the right words. "There's g-gossip."

"And have people treated you differently?"

Jed rocked back in his chair. Certainly some of them gawked at him like he'd grown a second head. Even his own family, apart from Mike and Hannah, had acted differently than before. Aside from his father's silences, they didn't shun him. But they didn't know how to act. Like learning he liked men had changed who he was to them.

"My f-family. I came out recently."

"And how did that go?"

The mirthless laugh ripped from his throat. "C-could have been b-better," he admitted. "I w-was angry. They w-were confused. It w-was ugly."

"Would you like me to set up family counseling? Allow you to meet in a neutral spot? I could facilitate the conversation."

"No. I . . . I don't w-want—" He paused. "Do you th-think it's w-wrong?"

"No." She shook her head vehemently. "You are exactly as God intended you to be. Love is not a sin."

"B-but I lied."

She winced. "You lied because you needed to protect yourself. Do you think God can't forgive that? I think that honesty is a wonderful thing—I think coming out is going to ultimately be good for you. But I don't believe waiting until you were ready is unforgiveable."

Her words tore open something in him. He took a deep breath, not sure he could put words to how much he'd needed to hear that.

"C-can . . . can you help me ex-explain? How do I . . . Pastor G-Green . . ."

"Do you know why Pastor Green left?"

He shook his head.

"In March, the presbyteries approved a change in church doctrine, defining marriage as 'between two people,' language which took effect in June."

Around the time Pastor Green's sermons about marriage had started to sound like something out of the 1950s.

"P-politics aren't m-my thing," he admitted. He knew there had been changes in church doctrines—they'd made the news—but he didn't ever expect them to touch down in Blandford.

She smiled. "No. Mine neither. Pastor Green has left the PCUSA, and joined the PCA—whose teachings adhere more closely to his own beliefs."

The air rushed out of Jed's lungs like he'd been punched in the diaphragm.

"I-I—" Tears pricked his eyelids.

"Jed, this church is your home. Your faith is as welcome here as it has always been."

The tears flowed freely then, and she handed him a box of tissues and waited patiently for him to collect himself. The weight of years of silence being torn away was painful—like blood rushing to a numb limb. It took several minutes before he could speak again.

"Th-thank you."

"Thank you for trusting me, Jed. And I meant what I said about facilitating family counseling for you, if that's something you'd like. I'm on your side."

"W-would it help?"

"It can't hurt."

Jed nodded. "L-let's try it."

That night, Jed opened a chat window on his computer and scrolled until he found Connor's avatar, a black-and-white headshot, the eyes Jed loved obscured by sunglasses, and that sexy bow mouth twisted into a sneer. The first time he'd seen it, Jed had laughed, because it was so unlike Connor. But after following Connor's Instagram account for a few weeks, he'd begun to see the other side of Connor, the cocky, pushy photographer who moved in the same world as the models he photographed. Jed was surprised how much *that* side of Connor turned him on too.

Hey, you around?

The reply was almost instant. *In a hotel in London. What's up?*

London. Jed had never been farther away than Washington DC. How many hours' time difference was there between Massachusetts and London? *Is it late there?*

Yeah. I don't mind. How is everything? Your family?

Jed smiled. Connor always asked. He never asked about his own brother, who Jed saw from time to time. But he always asked about Jed's.

They're okay. I met the new minister today. She's amazing. I'm hoping the family will join me for counseling with her.

It was the first time he had admitted to Connor that maybe everything wasn't *okay*. Since Connor's relationship with Scott was almost nonexistent, he'd felt guilty sharing his own family problems.

That's good—is a minister qualified to do that?

Not that kind of counseling—more like, just talking to each other with someone else to help when the conversation gets rough.

That's really good, Jed. I wish I'd had support like that. I hope it helps.

Jed wiped his eyes.

Do you think it's too late for you and Scott?

He didn't know why he'd asked that, except that he remembered Connor clutching him and crying in the attic, and that no matter how much he tried to play it off like it wasn't important, the estrangement hurt Connor.

Never say never, I guess. My phone battery is about to die. Text me tomorrow?

Jed frowned at his laptop screen, at the sneer and the sunglasses and the flippant reply hiding the hurt boy inside. He wanted to reach through that screen and hug Connor. How long was he going to be able to pretend that texts and chats and occasional visits were enough?

Of course. Miss you.

Miss you too. Only two more weeks. Can't wait. Good night, Jed. X

Chapter Twelve

J ed was nervous—crazy nervous—when he stepped off the L train in Williamsburg and took the steps up to the street, tugging his hood tighter against the falling snow. After what felt like an excruciatingly long train ride from Springfield, he was minutes from seeing Connor again and the dusting of snow felt like magic—a quiet blessing over the time they'd planned together.

His heart beat a little faster as he slung his bag over his shoulder.

It was ridiculous, right? To be so infatuated with someone he'd only spent a handful of days with, but for Jed, those handful of days had been brighter and more full of beauty than the rest of his life. And Connor had been there for him when he'd come out—had been the reason he could, even if the method had been impetuous and the timing terrible.

Connor had been there when he needed someone. Had held him when he cried. Had offered to sit and chat with him on the computer so Jed wouldn't have to stammer through his pain.

And the past three months, every time he texted Connor, the man had texted him back almost immediately—sometimes sweet, sometimes sexy enough to make him blush. Those conversations meant everything to Jed.

And they terrified him, because they weren't enough. He wanted Connor in his life every day, and he had no idea how to ask for that. Just the thought reminded him of all the ways he'd blown it with Kyle, and he was determined not to push too hard again.

He peeked at the address he'd long since memorized and trudged the few blocks until he found the building. The ground floor boasted retail space, and the first area was empty, but the next one over had the name of Connor's studio on the awning.

His phone buzzed. He tucked himself against the wall in the doorway to the studio and checked his texts. Connor.

Where are you?

He laughed. *Why, is your dick hard?*

He shivered as he waited for the answer.

Ask me again and the answer will be yes. Are you in the city yet?

Jed decided to take pity on him—and on his own freezing hands.

I'm outside, leaning against your building, thinking about your dick.

He waited for a text back, wondering how long Connor would keep up the conversation after that, but a text never came. Instead, Connor himself burst through the door with no hat or coat or common sense, but with an eager grin and a frantic, sloppy, up-against-the-wall kiss.

Tongues sliding, breath hitching, hands *everywhere.*

Someone walking by muttered something that might have been encouragement, or perhaps a slur, but Jed didn't care, because he had an armful of Connor, and they were kissing in the snow, and life was beautiful.

"I gotta get you inside. Need to feel your skin." Connor pulled out of the kiss and half dragged Jed into the building and up a flight of stairs. Jed didn't even have a moment to get an impression of the studio space, just that it was large and the stairs were at the very back of it, and then they were through a door to the apartment upstairs.

Kissing.

Rough—fists balled in shirtfronts.

Gentle—hands stroking faces.

Lusty—a thigh thrust between his legs and a dirty, dirty grind dick to dick.

Sweet—a whimper in the back of a throat, an answering sigh.

Kissing.

Kissing Connor.

"I can't believe you're really here." Connor caught his breath and dived in for another kiss. "God, you feel so good. Can we—?"

Blue eyes met Jed's, accompanied by a questioning smile.

"Y-y-yes."

And then Connor's hands were on his belt, unbuckling, shoving everything down, and Connor was on his knees.

Holy shit, my dick is in Connor Graham's mouth.

It wasn't the first time, no. But now he'd had months to anticipate. Oh, they'd texted all kinds of filthy things to each other. They'd teased each other, and Connor had promised him a "legendary blowjob" to welcome him to the city. Jed had been curious—just what would make a blowjob legendary? His ideas had fueled so many jerk-off sessions.

But Jed's imagination hadn't done the thrill of Connor's lips on his cock justice. Anticipation had only heightened the sensations of Connor's tongue tracing the vein, teasing under the head and circling. The way he sucked like he wanted to unravel Jed's brain right through his dick was better than anything from Jed's fantasies.

The world fell away, leaving nothing but Connor's hot mouth, his throat working as he tried to take Jed all the way inside. Connor's hand between his legs, cupping his balls, giving just the right amount of pressure. Connor groaning, the vibration sliding along Jed's cock like a current.

"Oh my word." Jed's hips thrust, and Connor gagged a little, but held tight and wouldn't let Jed pull away.

The promise of bliss built in his balls, climbed his spine, and seemed to curl outward from his dick.

"C-c-coming," he choked out, and Connor took him even deeper into his mouth, practically growling around his dick as he did, and slid the tip of one finger over Jed's hole with decadent, dirty promise.

Jed shouted incoherently as he shot into Connor's mouth. Connor swallowed the first bit, then pulled off, pumping the shaft with one hand and licking the head, letting the spurts of cum splash on his cheek like it was the most wonderful thing in the world. And when Jed sank back against the door, Connor lunged to his feet and kissed him. Slow, salty kisses that tasted like Jed and like Connor and like love.

Jed reached into Connor's sweatpants and found him hard and straining.

"Oh god, yes, please, I need— Gah!" Connor's hands braced on the door, one on either side of Jed's head as he watched Jed jerking him. "So hot, honey."

Jed loved it when Connor praised him. Loved it when Connor whined in the back of his throat like that. Loved when he panted like he'd run a mile when Jed squeezed just so.

When Jed added a twist to his wrist as he jerked, Connor came unglued, babbling sweet, gorgeous nothing-words until he shuddered and came. Hot liquid coated the back of Jed's hand, and he brought it up for a taste, and then they were kissing again, and laughing, and straightening clothes, and wiping hands and faces and trying not to blush.

"So." Connor rubbed the back of his neck and grinned at Jed. "Can I take your coat?"

That first night in New York, they stayed in and it was a blur of sex and sleepy kisses, a pizza delivery and eating at 3 a.m. in their underwear. Connor couldn't believe Jed was really here, and kept touching him to reassure himself that the man in his bed was real. When Jed smiled, all soft and sated with kiss-bruised lips and stubble burn on his throat, Connor's heart felt like it would thud right out of his chest.

"Again?" Jed teased.

Connor shook his head. "Just don't want to stop touching you."

Jed stretched and pulled Connor's head onto his shoulder. "T-touch me as much as you w-want."

"I want to talk too. I jumped you the minute you walked in and we haven't come up for air."

"M-making up for lost time." Jed's smile fell a bit, and he rolled his head away.

"Hey, where'd you go?" Connor whispered.

Jed turned back to him and smiled again, but this time there was something forced about it. "Nowhere."

Connor let it slide.

"Where do you want to go tomorrow? Did you want to do any sightseeing? I'm the worst tour guide ever, but if there's something you want to see . . ."

Some of the light came back to Jed's smile. "I'm here for y-you. But I w-wouldn't mind seeing an urban farm. I st-studied them, you know. Never saw one in person."

"I'll call around in the morning."

"I th-think it is the morning." Jed rolled him onto his back and kissed him deep and slow like they had all the time in the world. "B-but call later."

Connor had made reservations for Thanksgiving dinner at a neighborhood restaurant he called "dressy, bring a suit."

Jed only had his church suit. It was medium-gray wool, and boring, and he was pretty sure it wasn't in style, but it was all he had. So when Connor stepped out of the bathroom in a perfectly fitting dark-gray suit that seemed to shine a little, with a purple shirt and a vibrant blue tie, Jed's heart sank.

"Whoa, what's that frown for?" Connor sat down on the bed with him. "Don't like purple? Is my tie too bright?"

Jed shook his head. "You're per-perfect. I'm g-gonna look like such a hick."

Connor's eyes widened. "You're kidding me, right? Have you seen yourself in the mirror?"

Jed stood, unzipped his bag, and held up his suit. Yep, still boring.

Connor smiled. "Okay, it's not the fanciest suit, but it's a classic style. And if that's the one you wore to church, I know it's well tailored. Wear it without a tie and every queer in the city is going to want your number."

Jed scoffed, but Connor pulled him into the bathroom and pointed to the mirror.

The bathroom smelled like Connor's soap and was still filled with steam, but Connor wiped the mirror with one hand and then held Jed's shoulders.

"Your hair—you probably get it cut at Great Clips or something and it still looks better than an $80 haircut. You have amazing hair. It's thick and soft and every time I look at you I want to bury my hands in it." Which he did, and kissed Jed until they were both breathing heavily.

"Your eyes are really nice—such a gorgeous shade of brown, and so serious looking, but I know they're hiding a wicked sense of humor. Your lips—well. Let's just say I have jerked off many times thinking about those lips." Connor grinned. "But this?" He tilted Jed's chin. "That day we met, I saw this jawline, and I asked to photograph you right then and there because you have the sexiest, *sexiest* fucking jaw I've ever seen. And when you walk into that restaurant, all you have to do is jut your chin just so, and no one will give a fuck that your suit isn't some four-thousand-dollar custom Italian job."

Jed blushed, laughing. "My j-j-jaw?"

Connor kissed the back of his neck and bit, a sharp little nip where his shoulder and neck met.

"Yeah, your fucking jaw gets me hard, okay?"

Jed turned and looped his arms over Connor's neck. "I just w-w-want to be a g-guy you're pr-proud to be with."

"Never doubt it. Ever."

The pep talk went a long way toward easing the fish-out-of-water sensation for a while, but as he soaped himself in the shower, the doubts crept back in. Connor treated him the way he always dreamed a lover would. He took the time to make Jed feel wanted and cherished. He was kind and considerate—had even managed to get them in to see a rooftop farm, though it was closed to the public for the winter, in exchange for some publicity photographs come spring time.

He treated Jed like the most important person in his life, but a hundred and fifty miles away, a For Sale sign hung on the property that had brought them together, and Connor never acknowledged that the pending sale was still between them. Jed had fantasized about Connor coming home, moving back to Blandford and making a life with him. Now he felt silly and childish for indulging in that fantasy, even for a second. He turned the taps off and leaned against the wall as the air cooled around him.

What was he doing here? A weekend fling? A booty call?

Where did he fit into Connor's life outside of the bedroom or the farm? Jed knew better than to push for more than a lover could give—but he and Connor, they were *good* together. Here in the city, that was even clearer to him. At home, they'd been the only gay men in town—and he'd been able to fool himself that only novelty and common ground had brought them together. Now he couldn't lie to himself and say it was still convenience and mutual attraction. This was affection and a choice to be together. And he wanted Connor to keep choosing him.

As they approached the restaurant later, Jed had his second case of nerves. He stopped Connor with a hand on his arm. "I-I n-need you to ord-order for me."

Connor smiled. "It's a fixed menu. I'll order the wine. You like red or white?"

Relief washed over Jed. "B-both."

A dinner out hadn't been this easy in years. It seemed that Connor didn't expect him to talk, but when he did, Connor listened and didn't once interrupt him or talk over him. He could relax, which helped him stammer less.

"D-do you ever think you'll move back?" he finally got up the courage to ask as they finished the main course.

Connor stilled. "To Blandford?"

Jed took a bite of his turkey and nodded. "You seemed to love the farm. Your p-paintings. I just w-wondered if you ever . . ."

"No. It's not home anymore. Just a place I used to know, you know?"

Flinching inwardly, Jed hid his disappointment behind another nod and a sip of his wine. He'd only meant to feel Connor out on the subject, but had managed to shut it down instead. That no had sounded pretty definitive. He tried to imagine the only alternative: himself, here in Brooklyn. He fell silent again, thankful for once that his stutter allowed him an excuse to keep quiet. Yeah, he could see it. The fantasy sent a sharp-bright thrill through him, and for a second he let it gain momentum—that he was here not for a weekend, but for a lifetime. That this was the first of many holiday dinners they would share. But that was impossible too, because even though the crop was in for the season, they were both still tied to the farm—Connor to its land value, and Jed to its crop for the next two years. The farm's ability to draw them together was only outmatched by its ability to keep them apart.

Connor didn't seem to notice Jed's withdrawal, and returned their mostly one-sided conversation back to lighter topics. When dessert arrived, Jed dug in, desperate for distraction—anything to tear his mind from his stupid hopes and how easily they broke.

Chapter
Thirteen

Jed had a hard time reconciling his emotions on the way home. Holding hands with Connor was weird, awkward, and somehow still exhilarating as they strolled down the street where anyone could see. He couldn't quite wrap his head around the idea that this was him, Jed Jones, walking with his lover. The ease of it made him feel like a stranger even to himself. All those years in the closet, sneaking around, had taken their toll on him, made him believe he wasn't the kind of guy to hold hands, but walking with Connor, Jed couldn't imagine it any other way.

Talking about an art show he wanted to do once he opened the gallery next door to his studio, Connor gestured wildly with his free hand. He was so animated, so excited, in a way he hadn't seemed to be in Blandford.

The certainty that Connor would never, ever leave the city rolled over Jed like a tsunami, and he stumbled.

"You okay?" Connor asked.

Jed nodded, facing him again, blinking hard and smiling, even though he'd just broken his own heart. How had he ever thought he could ask Connor to abandon this for him? But how could he settle for being squeezed into Connor's life, a weekend here or a weekend there? No promises, no commitments? And how could he let Connor know he might want more than that without being too demanding? Echoes of his relationship with Kyle left a bitter taste in his mouth.

Connor spoke first. "Hey, do you want to go dancing?"

"D-do you?"

Connor stopped and glanced at him, a curious expression on his face. "I don't, actually. But I thought you might . . ." He shoved his hand in his pocket and blushed. "I was trying to think of things we could do where you wouldn't have to talk if you didn't want to."

Jed shook his head. Connor was always trying to make life easier for him. The fixed menu dinner. Text messages instead of phone calls. Letting him email his thoughts on just about anything, and replying as if it was normal to communicate that way with someone in the next room. Jed pushed away his worries about the future and squeezed Connor's hand.

"I w-want to g-go home with you. And we d-don't need to t-talk."

A wicked smile spread across Connor's face. "Can I photograph you?"

Jed laughed. "If you w-want."

His sense of anticipation heightened as Connor let them in through the studio, gesturing upstairs.

"Go ahead up. I just want to grab a few things I'll need from down here."

"You d-don't w-want . . . ?" Jed glanced around the studio space. Connor had given him a tour that morning, showing off the floor-to-ceiling windows on the back wall, and the various sets he had staged for shooting models. He'd even given Jed a quick—albeit cold—tour of the roof, where he'd shot an album cover for a band. It had been the vacant space next door he'd really been excited about though.

"This is going to be a gallery." He'd whispered it with the kind of reverence Jed reserved for church.

Connor was so proud of this studio he'd made, so why didn't he want to photograph Jed in it?

He smiled like he knew what Jed was thinking. "I work here. I want these shots to be personal. Intimate. I want to photograph you in my home."

Jed swallowed. *Intimate.* His heart may have shattered on the sidewalk outside, but it still found a way to beat a little faster at that word. Nodding, he went upstairs.

He hung his overcoat from the coat hook inside the door, then stood in Connor's kitchen, unsure what to do next. Should he change clothes? Get naked? *Intimate.*

The waiting was going to kill him. It wasn't until Connor finally came through the door, smiling—all round-cheeked and lit up with eagerness—that Jed's butterflies calmed.

Connor slid something into place on top of his camera. "A trigger, for the flash."

"F-flash?"

Connor held it up. "It's got a receiver on it. Wherever it is in the room, it will flash when I take the photo. So I can turn any wall or ceiling or window shade into my light source. But first . . . Here."

He set down the camera and flash, hung up his coat and jacket, yanked off his tie, and rolled up his sleeves with brisk efficiency.

Pulling Jed to him by the lapels, he kissed him hard. The contrast between the competent professional of a moment ago and the passionate lover shoving Jed back against the door made Jed's skin buzz with arousal. Connor pressed their bodies tight together and grabbed a fistful of Jed's hair. It was *hot*. Intense, rough, and yes, *intimate*. Jed groaned, and Connor bit his lower lip and sucked, then let him go.

"Yeah." Connor reached for his camera and flash while Jed's chest was still heaving. The flash was pointed at the wall when it briefly, brilliantly, illuminated them both. It whined as it recharged. Then again.

Flash, whine.

"Unbutton your shirt, slowly."

Flash, whine.

Jed did as he was told, their breathing and the click of the shutter loud in the small space.

"Your hands. Holy— Stop. Stop right there."

Jed waited, a button half-slipped through a hole.

Flash, whine. Flash, whine.

"Give me your jacket."

Jed let Connor yank it from his shoulders, and he stood there, shirt open almost to the waist, dick achingly hard in his pants as he waited for Connor to tell him what to do next. But Connor didn't. He wrapped his arm around Jed and seduced him with another kiss. A long, slow, drugging kiss that traveled from lips to ear to jaw and ended with a nip at the hollow of his throat.

"You're k-killing me."

"When you go home, I'm not gonna be able to kiss you like this. But I can take out these pictures, and see you all kiss-drunk and sexy.

And I can remember how good you tasted and how nice it was to have you here, and that will tide me over until next time."

Jed went limp against Connor. There couldn't be an endless string of next times, and he knew it. But Connor's words still excited him, still turned him on, still made him want to make the most of *this* time.

"Come on, let's go to bed."

Jed followed Connor to the little bedroom, let him take the rest of his clothes off between languid, lush kisses and soft moans. A hand found his hard cock and stroked it, slow and strong. Fluid welled in his slit, and Connor spread it along the shaft, making him arch and gasp.

"Lie down, hold the sheet over your legs and dick." Connor picked up his camera again.

Jed hesitated, but only for a moment. If this was something he could give Connor, he would do it. He pulled the sheet—a luxurious Egyptian cotton in solid gray—up until it covered his cock.

"Yeah, like that. Prop your head up on your hand. Remember what I said about your jaw? Gorgeous." Connor positioned the flash so it pointed at the corner, then he made an adjustment to his camera and the flash-whine chorus started again.

Jed watched Connor, limbs leaden with lust. The cool, calm efficiency with which Connor worked was in sharp contrast to his heavy-lidded gaze and shallow breath. At one point, Connor pressed a hand over his own cock, letting out a quiet moan. The sound provoked an answering moan from Jed.

When Connor told him to, he rolled over onto his stomach. Folding his arms under his chin, he tried to steady his breathing as Connor drew the sheet down and away.

He was exposed. Naked and exposed, not just for his lover, but for the camera. A flush rose over his skin.

"Raise your right knee a little, just a lit— Oh god, your ass."

Jed peered over his shoulder at that, a small smile tugging at the corners of his lips. Connor might love bottoming, but apparently he appreciated the sight of Jed's ass.

"Don't move."

Flash, whine. Flash, whine. Flash, whine.

"You c-can f-fuck me." Jed's voice came out strangled, but he meant it. He wanted to feel Connor move inside him at least once. He didn't know if he'd like bottoming—he'd never been much interested in trying it before—but he wanted to know what made Connor beg him for it in that rough voice, and he wanted to know badly enough to ignore his nerves.

Connor set the camera aside.

"Yeah? You want that? Or just saying it because I'm making gaga eyes at your ass?"

"W-w-want it. Want you."

Connor started shedding his clothes, fast. Jed laughed as he watched, and then Connor was over him in the bed, biting the back of Jed's neck, then kissing his way down Jed's spine. Teeth, tongue, lips, all worked to diminish Jed's nerves.

"It feels good, I promise," Connor murmured between kisses. "It might hurt a little, but then I'm going to make you feel so good. Open your legs for me."

Jed did. He'd thought it would be embarrassing, having another man gazing at his ass like this. But there was no shame, only a thrilling vulnerability, when Connor made those low, sexy noises in his throat and touched him so gently.

At first, he just stroked his fingers over Jed's hole, barely a whisper of sensation, until Jed relaxed, and then the rub became harder, more intense.

"Would you freak out if I rimmed you?"

The question surprised Jed, and he shuddered in anticipation. He shook his head.

Connor lifted Jed's ass, spreading him at the same time. Jed groaned into the pillow as he felt first Connor's lips, then his tongue.

It was magic. How had he gone well into his fourth decade thinking an occasional blowjob or handjob from a chat-room hookup was satisfying enough? How had he convinced himself that dating women and hiding behind a veneer of heterosexuality was any way to go through life? Letting Connor see him turned on and vulnerable and needy? This was *intimate*.

He let go of any ideas that this act was dirty or embarrassing. How could he be embarrassed when he trusted Connor this much? Jed's body was suddenly hot and tingling like every nerve was connected to that one tender place where Connor was spearing into him. His dick ached and his balls tightened. He didn't know how long Connor devastated him with lips and tongue, only that by the time Connor poured lube on his fingers and slid one into Jed, he'd never needed a touch so badly.

Jed arched, flinching away from the invasion—oh God, *penetration*. But then Connor kissed him low on the back and he relaxed. It was . . . good. And when Connor added more lube, and started moving that finger, even better.

Jed dropped his head forward, and he pushed back. Connor's finger moved deeper, probed, and then— Holy shit. He was going to come, a sudden well of pressure in his groin, and he wasn't ready, *not yet*. But then the pressure moved away and he was left stunned and gasping for more.

"W-what?"

"Prostate," Connor said. "It feels good, right? Some guys can come just from that. Though, some guys don't like it."

"I l-like it." Jed pushed back again, and Connor added more lube and started pressing a second finger inside him.

Jed tensed—Connor's fingers were thick—but Connor ran a soothing hand down his side. "Relax, it'll feel so good."

And it did. It really, really did. The fingers brushed Jed's prostate, more gently, purposefully. A caress, or a massage even. Jed's hips started moving. He ground his dick into the sheets and then his ass onto those fingers. Connor wasn't kidding; it was fucking *amazing*. Was he one of those guys who could come just from ass-play? He didn't know. But between the ass-play and the friction on his cock, he was definitely going to explode.

"G-g-gonna . . ." The fingers slipped away, and Connor's body moved over his.

"You tell me if anything hurts. I'll go slow, okay?"

Jed nodded, but deep down, he didn't care if it hurt. He only knew he needed Connor to touch him, fuck him, make him come.

Blunt pressure breached him, and he groaned low and long. Connor nipped at his shoulder, and paused.

"C-come *on*," Jed grunted, pushing, and Connor slid forward, so Jed pushed harder, and then Connor was inside him all the way.

"God, you . . . you feel—" Connor thrust again and it shook Jed all the way to his heart.

"M-m-more."

Connor was gentle with him, moving slowly, lifting Jed's hips so he could work his cock as they fucked. "You're so sexy, Jed. I love seeing you like this. All hot for me. Love the way it looks where I'm sliding into you." The filthy litany of half praise, half narration spilled from Connor's lips in a constant stream. "You wanna know what the best part is? The best part is knowing how good it feels when you do this to me, and knowing that I'm making you feel good like that. Seeing how hard you are, how much you want this."

Jed flushed, because he did; he wanted this. More than naked, he felt *seen*. Not just physically vulnerable, but emotionally bare—how else could Connor know exactly why he'd wanted to share this? Connor understood him better than anyone else he'd ever known. He rocked back harder into Connor's movements, and they found a rhythm together, steady and intense, that had Jed crying out and speeding his hand on his cock.

"C-close."

"Yeah, wanna see you come." Connor fucked him harder, fingers digging into hips, and Jed lost it. He came so hard he thought he'd pass out. Connor shouted, and the sound drew another spurt from Jed's now oversensitive dick.

Connor withdrew as carefully as he'd driven in, and collapsed to the bed next to Jed, pulling him into strong arms.

"So good," Jed gasped. "I never knew."

"I love it when you do it to me, but god, that's fun too."

Jed grinned. "Yeah." The word came out around a yawn.

"I have to admit, I never thought I'd get to do this with you. I know it was terribly prejudiced of me, but when you said you were religious, I figured you'd be all puritanical about sex."

Jed snorted and sighed sleepily. "Everybody fucks, Con."

He yawned again and drifted to sleep in Connor's arms.

When Jed woke up, Connor was snoring softly, and dawn was barely touching the edges of the sky outside the window. He knew this couldn't last indefinitely, but he resented that sunrise. He resented the fact that it would rise again on Saturday. And again on Sunday, when he would have to leave. He resented that pending separation even as he pulled Connor closer, and snuggled his face into that warm place where neck met shoulder.

Connor wiggled, ass bumping right up into Jed's groin, and wrapped Jed's hand in his own. Jed loved how easy it was to take his fill of touch with Connor. Loved being with Connor. Maybe even was starting to love Connor himself.

Ah, who was he kidding? Starting to? He'd let the man photograph him naked and fuck him senseless. Those weren't the kinds of things he would do with just anyone. Those were trust things. Love things. He was gone over this guy.

Which made it even harder, knowing that he couldn't keep him forever. Connor would stay in New York, and Jed would stay in Blandford. Seeing each other for a weekend here or there with no commitments or promises wasn't enough. Not for Jed.

But they had today, and tomorrow. So he did the only thing he could do: held his man tighter and woke him with a long, desperate kiss.

Connor couldn't help but feel like Jed was retreating from him over the weekend. By Sunday, the silences between them had gone from comfortable to strained, though he couldn't put his finger on why. Jed sat on Connor's bed, apparently lost in thought. His bag was packed, sitting by the front door, his train reservation tucked safely inside.

Even brooding and distant, Jed was beautiful. Desperate to capture one of these last fleeting moments of the weekend, Connor grabbed the camera from the dresser and snapped a photo. Jed offered a smile—a fake, for-the-camera smile.

"You seem really preoccupied this morning."

"I can't d-d-do this."

Connor's heart sank, but he tried for levity anyway. "Can't do what? Leave? Don't then, stay forever."

He said it teasingly, but now, with the invitation hanging between them, he wished he hadn't made a joke of it.

Jed's smile didn't reach his eyes. "I c-can't-can't keep s-s-s—" He took a breath. "Seeing y-you."

All the air was sucked out of the room; Connor fought to reorient himself.

This wasn't how the weekend was supposed to end. It wasn't supposed to end *them*. It was the first in what he'd hoped would be lots of visits. The beginning of a relationship. How could he have read it so wrong?

"Why not? If anything this just proved how easy it is to make time to get to the city. And it was fun, right?" He couldn't be the only one who had fun. Connor searched his brain for the moment things had changed—had he come on too strong? Where had he fucked up?

Jed nodded. "I meant w-what I said. No regrets. N-not you."

"But you're breaking it off—why? Whatever I did, I'll make it up to you."

Jed opened Connor's laptop, pulled up a blank document, and began to type furiously. Connor sat on the bed and watched over his shoulder.

I mean it. I don't regret you. I don't regret the weekend. But I can't keep doing this. I'm not a pieces and parts of a life kind of guy. I couldn't do that for Kyle. And I don't think I could settle for that from you. But I can't sit here and demand something of you that you can't give me. Your life, your work, your home is here. Mine is back in Blandford. And I'm bound, legally and financially, to that work—to making your land profitable. I have this fantasy of buying out the farm and you moving in with me, and us living out our lives like that—like family. But that's my fantasy. I think it took seeing you here, seeing how your brightness and your art and your everything fits here to realize you can't be happy living the life I live. And I won't ask you to. I want more than that for you. And for me. I ju

"Jed, stop. Stop." Connor pulled the laptop out of his hands and set it aside. His gut churned as he cast about for some solution, some quick fix. Jed wanted a *life* together. In *Blandford*. Moving back to Blandford was impossible—it would kill his career. But the life together part? That was impossibly tempting. Connor wanted *that*.

Wanted Jed in his home and his life like family. Couldn't they find a compromise? He wrapped his arms around Jed and held him tightly. "Stop, please stop."

Tears stung his eyes.

"I'm s-s-sor-sorry." Jed pillowed his head on Connor's shoulder and clutched him right back, his tears flowing freely into Connor's shirt. "D-don't w-w-want to hurt you."

"So don't. Don't hurt either of us. We can make it work, can't we? Find middle ground?"

"W-we can't, Con."

"Why not? Why does it have to be all or nothing?"

Jed groaned and pushed Connor away. "Because I'm s-selfish. I need m-more than you can give me." He stood and straightened his shoulders like he was shrugging off their entire connection.

"You aren't— For fuck's sake, Jed, don't make what we have small."

But Jed's expression had shut down.

"W-w-we can be fr-friends. I'd l-like that."

"Do you know how much it's going to hurt when all I can have of you is liking your Facebook statuses?"

"I c-c-can't be your w-w-weekend boyfriend."

"But I—*we* could find a way to make it work, right? There's got to be something we can do." *Please don't walk away from me.*

"Know of any f-farmland for s-sale?"

And there it was. Jed needed plants like Connor needed art. Farming wasn't just work he did. It was him, a part of him, a vocation, in the kind of man who believes in higher callings. A connection to his community. He had that in Blandford, and Connor didn't know how to give him that, here.

"So, we're friends." Connor struggled to say the words, but Jed nodded.

"If it d-doesn't hurt t-too much."

"It hurts."

"I'm s-sorry. I don't w-w-want . . ." Jed sniffed and rubbed a hand across his eyes. "I underst-stand if you don't want to be friends."

Connor wanted to scream. Instead he took several deep breaths and tried to piece himself back together. "I can try."

"I don't— I don't want to say g-good-bye at the train. Want it to be pr-private."

Connor pulled himself together enough to give Jed a long, steady hug.

"I feel like I should be kissing you," he confessed.

Jed made a noise that wasn't quite a laugh or a sob, but maybe something in between. He drew back and stared right into Connor's eyes—there was so much strength, so much determination, and so much sadness in that gaze. And then Jed smiled and kissed him, hard, quick, too quick to respond.

"Good-b-bye, Con."

After Jed left, Connor stared out the window for a while. Then he gave up and climbed into bed—which still smelled like Jed—and he cried until he felt empty.

Chapter
Fourteen

The envelope that showed up in the mail was big, made from heavy cardboard, and bore a New York return address. It was the second week in December, only weeks after he'd left Connor, and Jed wasn't quite sure enough time had passed that he was ready to see the contents of the photo mailer.

"photos. do not bend." was written in Connor's blocky scrawl, even though it was also printed on the envelope itself. Jed took the envelope inside the farmhouse and sat down at the dining room table.

He read the note first.

Jed—

I don't know if this is fair to you. But I wanted you to have the same souvenirs of our weekend as I do. Every one of these is beautiful to me, and I printed all of them twice except for the last one. I can't look at that one without wanting to scream. You have the only copy there in your hands. I'm going to Italy in January. I wish I could bring you with me. I'm so mad at you, but mostly I just miss you.

Yours,
Connor

Jed's hands shook as he pulled out the first photo. He barely recognized himself. His hair was messed up from Connor tugging on it. His lips dark from being bitten. In black and white, his shirt was crisp under his suit, the open collar baring the skin of his throat. His Adam's apple stood out like sculpture, and his eyes . . . his eyes, staring directly into the camera at Connor, were the eyes of a man who would give anything to have the object of his focus.

The next few photos, also in black and white, were more abstract. Pieces of him. His fingers pushing a button through its hole. His jaw. His chest.

And oh, God, his ass. He took the photo from the pile and looked more closely.

His body stretched out in Connor's bed, round globes of his ass lit softly, one leg raised. His face just peeking back over his shoulder, like he was inviting someone to take him—and wasn't that what he'd done? But it was more than that. He blushed at the memory of Connor inside him. Connor making love to him. Showing him how much pleasure there was in everything they could do together. His heart burned, and there was a lump in his throat. This must be exactly what Connor had wanted him to feel when he sent that note. This ache so deep, longing so sharp. "*The same souvenirs.*"

The last photo was the morning he left. There he was, sitting on Connor's bed, a strained, fake smile on his face. The morning he'd told Connor he didn't want to hurt him, though he'd known every word was a knife, and he was cutting deep and deadly. It made him want to scream. He stuffed the pictures back in the envelope, but gently folded the note and tucked it into his chest pocket, over his heart. Then he hid the photos away in his desk drawer, and tried to pretend he'd never seen himself through Connor's eyes.

The phone rang, and Jed flinched. Everyone in his life knew better than to call him, so it was likely a telemarketer. He let it go to voice mail, and then listened—the message was from the broker who handled his farm lease.

"Hello, Mr. Jones. This is Tom Harris. I got a phone call today from the lawyer handling Bruce Graham's estate. The Grahams have . . . Well. They have an offer on the farm, and I'd like to talk to you about it. I know you don't like to talk on the phone, so you can have that little lady who works for you call, or you can text me at this number."

Connor was going to get his gallery. That thought warmed Jed. But why would the broker need to talk to him about the offer? He didn't have any say in it. And any sale would be contingent on his lease for the next two years.

He texted.

You can call me back. Just don't expect me to talk much.

The phone rang again, and he picked up. "Hel-hello."

"Hi there, Mr. Jones. I hope you're well." Tom's voice was warm and gruff. "Now listen, there's a tenant buyout contingency on this offer, otherwise I wouldn't bother you."

Tenant buyout. Jed's heart seemed to stop, then patter faster than ever. Lease buyout on an agricultural property? It was unusual, but he knew his rights—he didn't have to agree to it. But if he didn't, would he just be prolonging the inevitable while standing between Connor and the gallery? And for what? The duration of his lease? Another two seasons?

"H-h-how early?"

There was a long pause. "The buyer wants to close within thirty days. Do you want to talk about numbers?"

Jed laughed, bitter and strangled. He'd have to find a job and somewhere else to live—and the last thing he wanted was to ask his family to take him in. Thirty-five years old and announcing he was homeless for Christmas? That would go over about as well as his coming out had. He dug the heel of his hand into his eyes.

"G-g-go ah-head."

Tom outlined the proposed terms of the tenant buyout offer. It was fair—and included ample payment for the expenses he'd already incurred for next year's harvest. He might be able to find a place to live before closing without having to resort to asking his parents if he could move back into their tiny home.

"The market for agricultural property isn't great right now, so I'm sure you can imagine the Grahams are anxious to respond."

"C-can I have some t-time?"

"Of course. Call me tomorrow, let me know where we stand. Take care, Mr. Jones."

Jed set the phone down and put his head in his hands, trying to calm his jumpy heart. A single day seemed hardly long enough to make a decision that would change his life.

That night, when a knock sounded on the farmhouse door, Jed figured it was one of his brothers come to borrow something, though why they wouldn't text ahead, he didn't know. But when he opened the door, it wasn't *his* brother, but Connor's, standing on the steps.

"Sc-Scott?"

"Jedidiah, you can't screw this up for me. I won't let you screw this up for me, you understand?" The man lurched forward like he was going to grab Jed, and when Jed took a step back, Scott stumbled, catching himself on the doorframe. He gasped and straightened—he looked like hell.

"Are you dr-drunk?"

"Only a little bit. Please, Jedidiah, you can't screw this up. Please."

Jed didn't want the man in his home. But he couldn't leave him out in the cold, drunk. People *died* in the snow. "Come in the house, Scott. We'll talk inside."

He opened the door wide, gesturing for Scott to sit on the sofa in the living room to their left. "C-coffee?"

Scott blinked at him. *'Only a little bit'? Yeah right.* "Got any beer?"

Rolling his eyes, Jed went to the kitchen and sent a quick text to Connor while he started the coffee.

Your brother is here.

Connor's text came back instantly.

Scott? Why?

Jed glanced in the living room, saw Connor's brother pacing instead of sitting.

IDK. He's drunk. What do I do?

His phone rang.

"Hel-hello?"

"You don't have to talk. Just put me on the phone with him." Connor's voice was so welcome, Jed almost wanted to keep him on the phone longer. But Connor was right. He walked back into the living room and handed Scott the phone. "C-Connor."

"Con, man, you have to tell your boyfriend not to screw this up for me."

Jed's back went ramrod straight. *Boyfriend?* Apparently the gossip mill had decided to sink their teeth into his business. Too bad they got it wrong. Small town, small minds. Two queers in the same room, must be love. Except—they weren't so wrong, were they?

"I just wanted to talk to him. Explain things." Scott had finally sat down, and was speaking in a rushed, almost-panicky voice. "I've got debts, Connor. And do you know how much divorce lawyers cost? I need this sale to go through."

Jed couldn't hear Connor's words, but he could hear his exasperated voice through the phone line.

"But you don't understand." Scott choked on the words like he was about to cry. "You've got loads of money, this isn't make or break for you."

Jed winced. Was Scott's financial solvency hanging on his decision too? His own financial solvency was enough of a worry, he didn't need this. Hell, he didn't even *like* Scott.

"I wouldn't hurt him! I just wanted to talk to him. What kind of person do you think I am?" Scott frowned up at Jed. "I didn't mean to scare you. I'm sorry."

Jed gave a tight nod. Connor had probably told him to say it, but it was something, anyway.

"No, I don't want to call Danny. No. Because if he hears I was out here with Jones, he'll think I'm queer. No offense. I can drive. Yes, I can."

Jed shook his head. Like that's the only reason anyone would visit him? Although Scott's friends weren't much more evolved than Scott, so maybe they would think that. Regardless, he didn't want Scott driving around drunk. He was the only family Connor had left.

"C-call Danny. Safer."

Scott glared up at him. "This isn't your business."

"Y-you're on my c-couch."

Scott had the sense to appear embarrassed. "Okay, I'll call him. Here." He thrust the phone back at Jed and reached in his pocket for his own.

Jed walked back to the kitchen. "Con?"

"Jesus, Jed, I'm sorry. And shit, I just did it again didn't I?"

Jed laughed. If they had kept seeing each other, would he have ever broken Connor of that habit? "Y-yeah. You d-did."

"He's calling his friend?"

"Y-yeah."

"Are you okay?"

Jed nodded, then realized Connor couldn't see him. "Yeah."

"Keep me on the phone until Danny gets there, okay? God, I miss you so much. Do you know how good it is to hear your voice?"

"D-don't, Con."

"I'm sorry. I'm sorry. I just . . . Don't you miss me at all?"

"Of c-c-c-course." Jed's emotions started to choke out his tongue. He hated how his stutter got worse the more important the words were. It was the cruelest thing.

"Did you get the pictures?"

"Y-yeah. Th-th-they . . ."

"You don't have to say anything. I just wanted you to see how gorgeous you are to me."

"Con."

"I know, I know. Is he still talking to Danny?"

Jed peeked into the living room, where Scott was standing at the window, peering out at the road. "No. He's w-watching."

"You know, if you said yes to the buyout, you could come stay with me."

Irritation flared in Jed that Connor would dangle the temptation of their relationship in front of him like that. Even so, the thought made his heart ache. Waking up in Connor's bed every morning was such an appealing fantasy. But that was all it could be, a fantasy.

"N-no, I c-couldn't. I'd just have to leave ag-g-gain."

"But listen, I had an idea, can you hear me out?"

Headlights swept across the windows. Scott's ride was here.

"G-gotta g-go. Danny's here."

He hung up. It sucked, hanging up on Connor. It was rude—the opposite of how he was raised, and it wasn't even what he wanted, but it was for the best—how could he go live with Connor while searching for another farm to lease? It would just end as badly as before.

At the door, Scott turned to him. "I'll come get my car tomorrow. Connor said he'd call the police if I bothered you, so I'll just come take it, right? He really likes you."

The bleary-eyed sincerity of a drunk.

"R-right."

When the door closed behind Scott, Jed locked it and turned the dead bolt.

Chapter
Fifteen

Connor stared at his phone. Well. He'd botched that hadn't he? He should have started with urban farming instead of "move in with me." And . . . oh god he hadn't actually said "move in with me." He'd planned to—and then in the moment he'd made it sound like he was offering a temporary respite rather than a new life together. He sighed and pulled out his laptop.

Dear Jed,

Look, I screwed that up. I'm sorry. When I'm excited, I get impulsive, and I say the wrong thing.

I know how important farming is, and I know you love what you do—that's part of what I admire about you—how you make things grow. Remember that farm we visited on the rooftop in Brooklyn? There are farms like that all over the city. You could grow things here. You could work for one of the farms, or get grants to start a new one. And I could help. I own the roof of my building, and the back of the gallery space is windowed—I don't know what it would take to convert it to a greenhouse, but I can ask my contractor for an estimate. It doesn't have to be my space. It could be ours.

You studied sustainable agriculture, and you worked Bruce's land. You could do this. I know it's a different world. I know I'm asking you to make a huge life change.

I don't want to take you away from something you love—you said you wanted more than I could give you. I want to give you everything. It's true, I need to live close to a major airport. But I'm self-employed. Even if I can't move to Blandford, I can visit. The town isn't the demon of my adolescent nightmares anymore.

I've seen how good the family therapy has been for you—and I want to help. I'll go to church with you when I can, and we can visit your family—whatever I can do to make you happy here.

When I said you could stay with me, what I meant was come live with me. Not as my weekend boyfriend. As my lover, my partner. Stay with me and never leave me.

Love,

Connor

He stared at the closing. Yeah, love. It felt good to put it in there, even if he wanted to say "I love you" for the first time in person. He took a deep breath and hit Send.

The conversation with Scott replayed in his mind. Scott had always had financial troubles off and on. Connor hadn't realized it was desperate, but it certainly explained some of Scott's paranoia over the summer. On an impulse, he called Scott back.

"Connor?" Scott slurred.

"Just wanted to— I just wanted to make sure you got home okay." Silence.

Connor waited a moment, then, "Scott? You're the only family I've got."

"I'm home. I'm fine." Scott's voice sounded strange. "Thanks." And he hung up.

Connor shook his head. Ah well, it had been worth a try.

Then he called his agent. "I don't think Italy is good timing for me. Can you give the job to the British kid with the pompadour?"

Jed read and reread the email several times. Urban farming. Rooftops and greenhouses. He'd studied it, but more as a curiosity than a real prospect—it seemed expensive and exciting, like something someone in a movie would do. Not Jed Jones from Blandford, Massachusetts.

But why not him?

He traced the last sentence with one finger. *Stay with me and never leave me.*

Connor had taken time from his glamorous life to think about ways they could be together, and both live their dreams—it was that important to him. Jed had thought maybe he would just—move on. That he hadn't? That he loved Jed and wanted him in Brooklyn—not for a weekend, but forever?

Stay with me and never leave me.

Jed was conflicted. He wanted that—he wanted it so much. But was it really possible? He would have some money from the lease buyout—enough to relocate, but not to live on in the city. He might have to work for someone else while he got started—a big urban farm would have foremen, right?

He opened a browser window and googled.

An hour later, he started writing down his experience—not a résumé exactly, but the bones of one. An hour after that, he began scribbling lists of organizations that provided grant funding to urban agriculture initiatives.

It was three in the morning before he finally went to bed, daring to hope. He pulled the sheets up to his chin and prayed like he hadn't since he was a child praying for his stutter to go away. He offered bargains and pleas, just like a child, but most of all, he whispered his hopes into the dark until he fell asleep.

The doorbell ringing woke him up.

Pulling a sweatshirt over his bare chest, he made his way downstairs to the front door, flung it open, and blinked. Hallucinating? Still asleep? He rubbed his eyes and blinked again.

"C-Connor?"

"Did I wake you up?" Connor smiled. "I'm sorry. I thought you'd be awake by now. You always woke early—before."

Jed scratched the back of his neck. "Y-yeah. Um. Late night. W-what are you doing here?"

Connor's face fell. "Did you get my email?"

Jed nodded. He tried not to stare, but after their weeks of separation, he was like a starving man at a feast, and Connor looked *good*. His cheeks were red from the cold, and his chin stubbled like he'd forgotten to shave. Sparkling blue eyes held the promise of that smile Jed loved so much.

"C-come on in." Jed gestured Connor inside.

Jed padded back toward the kitchen, and Connor followed. God, it was good to see him all sleepy-eyed and unguarded. Gone was the unease of that last day in New York, the distance that must have come from knowing he was going to break it off.

"C-coffee?"

"Sounds great."

Connor watched Jed fuss with the coffeepot. When he'd pressed Start, he turned and considered Connor like some puzzle he could solve if he just studied it long enough.

"How d-did you g-get here?"

Connor grinned. "I rented a car. Four-wheel drive—because of the snow. Can we talk about the email?"

Jed shoved away from the counter and stalked across the room, backing Connor up against the fridge. He stared down at Connor's lips, then right into his eyes as he leaned forward and pressed his mouth to Connor's.

Okay, so no talking. Connor could definitely get behind not talking.

He grabbed Jed's hips and pulled them up against his own, feeling Jed's cock stiffening in his sweats. Jed was kissing him roughly, like he couldn't get enough, sliding his tongue against Connor's and then nipping at his lips. Remembering how much Jed liked nipple-play, Connor slid his hands up under Jed's sweatshirt.

Jed squirmed, then laughed. "C-cold hands."

"Warm heart," Connor whispered, and then they were kissing again and he had his hands on Jed's nipples and Jed was making the best noises in his ears.

"B-bed?" Jed suggested, but Connor shook his head, instead dropping to his knees and pulling Jed's sweatpants down. God, he loved Jed's cock. He reacquainted himself by giving it a long slow lick up the length, then a kiss right at the tip.

"G-g-good, so good."

Connor smiled and took him deep. Jed's hands found his hair, tugged, then caressed, and Connor *loved* it. Looking up, he saw Jed's head thrown back, highlighting that sexy fucking jaw. He moaned around Jed's cock.

"St-stop." Jed shoved him away, not gently—frantically.

Connor sat back, chest heaving as he breathed hard. What had he done wrong? Grazed with his teeth? "I'm sorry."

"D-don't be. I almost came." Jed helped Connor to his feet and kissed him again. "Bed."

This time it wasn't a suggestion, and that was kind of hot too. They made their way up the stairs, fumbling with clothes and kissing the whole way. When they got to Jed's room, they fell on the bed, skin to skin, and Connor had never felt anything so good in his life.

"Do you want to fuck me?" he asked, a little breathless.

Jed shook his head, and lined their hips up, taking their cocks together in a callused hand. Oh, god, that was good. Jed fumbled next to the bed with his other hand, then produced a bottle of lube. He dumped some of it over their cocks and the slick friction had them both moaning and thrusting. Connor licked sweat from Jed's skin and groaned at the taste—a reminder that this wasn't just sex. It was Jed—impossible and essential.

He gave Jed his voice—his ragged groans and desperate pleas—and Jed pulled Connor right to the edge of his inevitable orgasm, then slowed his hand to stretch out their bliss. Connor rode that knife edge of anticipation until he was shaking from it, and then let the orgasm take him.

Struggling to catch his breath—aftershocks of pleasure still shook his body—he couldn't form a coherent thought. He was wrecked and rebuilt at once—Jed had a way of doing that to him. Even now, with his hands still on Connor's body, he was helping to put the pieces back together. Connor managed to collect himself enough to grip Jed's cock and to bite and lick along his jaw and whisper, "Come on, baby."

Jed followed a moment later, stuttering out Connor's name as his spine arched and cum splashed between them.

They lay there, stunned, for a long moment, then Jed was pulling blankets around them and smiling at him.

"Coffee can wait."

Connor smiled and snuggled close. "Can we talk now?"

"Yeah. I like talking *after* s-sex. Less stutter."

"Now, don't get me wrong, that was crazy hot and fun, but I'm getting mixed signals. I drove out here to talk, not to—" Connor gestured between them.

"I know. I just— It was like I was dr-dreaming, and you were there, and I couldn't help myself; I wanted you."

"What did you think of the email?"

Jed sighed, thrusting a hand into his bed-tousled hair. "I'm t-touched. And scared."

Connor's heart sank. "Scared doesn't sound good."

"W-wouldn't you be? If you were leaving every-rything you knew? I'm g-going to agree to the buyout. I'll call Tom today."

A wave of relief washed over Connor, and hope flared up. "And my proposal?"

"It w-was a proposal?"

Connor nodded, turning his head enough to nip a little bite on Jed's pec, just above his nipple. "It was."

"Then I accept."

"Really? You do?" Connor sat up, having to look into Jed's eyes.

He was smiling at Connor, and he nodded. "Really."

"You're moving to the city? You're gonna be a Williamsburg hipster urban farmer for real?"

"For r-real." Jed laughed. "It m-might take a while to sort out the f-farmer part. Can I be a hipster w-without a m-moustache?"

"Yes, but I'd love you even with a moustache." Connor kissed him.

Jed pulled out of the kiss and grinned, his face going all soft and sweet. "I love y-you too."

The coffeepot had shut itself off and the coffee was cold by the time they made their way back to the kitchen.

Chapter Sixteen

The next morning, it was Jed's turn to bring donuts to brunch, so he was last to arrive at Mom and Dad's, carefully trudging through the snow to the front door. The road conditions were bad, and only supposed to get worse, so he was planning to go back to the farmhouse as soon as brunch was over. After he'd come out, family meals had been strained, but they'd gotten better since they'd started counseling with Pastor Hopkins. His father was speaking to him again, and Luke and David had begun awkward forays into their previous brotherly teasing.

How would they take today's news? Connor had plans to visit Scott, so Jed was going to have to do this solo.

Hannah threw the door open and took the donuts while he stamped the snow from his boots. Had she been watching for him? Behind her, the kitchen was in full bustle.

"I heard about the offer on the farm. What are you going to do?" She murmured low so only he could hear.

He flinched. She'd be out of a job. Granted, she only worked during the busy season, but it was income, and she'd lose it. He'd been dreading this moment worst of all and she wasn't even giving him a chance to put it off.

"I'm s-sorry," he whispered back. "I'm go-going to New York."

"Don't be sorry, I'm happy for you." She put her hand on his arm and leaned even closer. "Also, I was waiting to tell you, but I'm pregnant. Due in July."

Relieved, he pulled her into a hug. "Cong-g-grats. Do they know?"

She shook her head. "You can break your news first, and Mike and I will cut in with ours if anyone acts disapproving."

"D-deal." Jed had really come to rely on his brother and his sister-in-law to help him relate to the rest of the family over the last few months. Luke and David had had a particularly hard time understanding that Jed had *always* been gay, but Mike and Hannah had supported him and stood up for him, and they were starting to find a new, hopeful normal.

Jed broke the news while saying grace, hoping the recitation of familiar prayer would hold his stutter at bay.

"Heavenly father, we give thanks for this food and pray that you bless it to the nourishment of our bodies. I pray that you keep my l-loved ones in health, and open their hearts to w-welcome another s-son and br-brother, my p-partner, Connor, as we begin a new life to-together. In Jesus's name, Amen."

The chorus of "Amens" that followed provided only the briefest respite before everyone started talking over one another. Hannah gave him a sly smile just before raising her voice to cut through the noise.

"Jed's gotten a buyout offer for his lease, isn't that right?"

"And I'm g-going to farm on rooftops in N-New York. Or t-try to."

"Jedidiah, you just decided a few months ago to be gay—" Luke started, but Mike interrupted.

"That's not how it works, dumbass."

"Language," Jed's dad said. He pinned Jed with a serious look, his brown eyes sharp and discerning. "Jed, your mother and I haven't had the easiest time understanding your lifestyle."

"Oh for heaven's sake, Dad, it's not a lifestyle it's an orientation, an identity," Hannah interrupted.

"Semantics." Dad waved her off. "Pastor Hopkins has helped us with this—a lot. I'm not a young man—change is hard, and admitting I may have wronged my child is harder. I want you to understand— I don't think who you *are* is wrong, but I don't approve of casual sexual relationships."

"Dad, ew!" Luke groaned. "And you said Jed coming out was inappropriate brunch conversation."

Dad leveled a glare on Luke that shut him right up; Jed hid a grin behind his napkin.

"You're a grown man—I'm not going to lecture you any further. You called him your partner, which I don't like as much as husband, but I'll deal with it. It wouldn't be fair to ask you questions I wouldn't ask your brothers. Does he make you happy?"

Jed smiled. "Yeah, Dad. He makes me w-wicked happy."

"And you can make a living—a real living—growing things on a roof?"

"Yes."

"I've always felt that you had a true calling. I would be sad to see you deny the work God gave you. If you can do that work with someone who loves you by your side, I will pray that he continues to make you happy, and perhaps someday, I'll feel comfortable to call him my son."

Tears prickled behind Jed's nose, but he held them back—heaven knew his brothers didn't need anything else to tease him about.

"Th-thank you."

"That's it? Guy says he's moving to New York to live with his gay lover and you're just cool with it?" David's jaw hung open. "You gave me a harder time about wanting to play football with the public-high-school kids."

Dad turned to David. "You were a child. He's a grown-up. You wanted to play a game. He wants to be with the person who makes him 'wicked happy.' I don't think the comparison is apt."

Mike cleared his throat. "I'm sure going to miss you this summer, man. I figured we could count on the baby whisperer again this time around."

And just like that, all the attention was on Mike. Jed grinned, taking the opportunity to snag a custard-filled donut.

Connor hadn't been to Scott's duplex since he'd moved to the city, but found it easily enough. The siding was in disrepair, and the roof sagged a bit over the porch, but other than that, it hadn't changed. He rang the bell and waited.

Scott came to the door, still in his Sunday church clothes. He glared at Connor through the storm door for a long moment, then opened it to let him in.

"Did you drive out three hours from the city just to lecture me about going to your boyfriend's house all drunk?"

Connor shook his head. "I drove out to talk him into being my boyfriend again."

Scott scowled.

"The sale's going through," Connor said. "I don't know if Marty called you. But Jed accepted the buyout."

"Yeah. Marty called."

Scott scratched at the back of his neck, then started removing his tie.

"You want a beer?"

Connor startled. Imagine that—his brother being almost human. "Um, no, thank you."

Scott disappeared into the kitchen, leaving Connor standing in the living room. When he returned, he waved the single beer in his hand as he spoke. "Well, you drove all this way, and apparently you've got *something* to say to me, or you wouldn't be here, so let's do this."

"You threatened my boyfriend." Rage boiled up in Connor, just like it had when Jed texted him that Scott was in his house.

Scott flinched. "Threatened? Listen, I'm really sorry if I scared him by going over there the other night. But I didn't mean for him to feel *threatened*. I was drunk, and I was scared."

"Don't *ever* do it again. You might have been a tough-shit football player, but I'm a decade younger and only made it out of high school alive because I could fight off guys bigger than you."

"Jesus, who knew the little queer had it in him," Scott sneered.

Connor pushed back the desire to punch the sneer right off his brother's face. "I'm leaving for New York tomorrow. And I'm coming back in January when we close on the farm. Jed's going to move in with me, so we're probably going to be in Blandford regularly to visit his family."

Scott scowled. "At least in New York, you won't be rubbing it in everyone's faces."

"Whose faces am I rubbing anything in? I'm a gay man. He's a gay man. We're in a relationship. You act like we're selling tickets to watch us fuck in Watson Park!"

"Gross." Scott took a swig of his beer.

"I'm the only family you've got. Why are you so fucking hostile all the time?" Connor shook his head. "Do you have any idea what it's like to know that I could have a fucking brother if he'd get his head out of his ass and act like one?" Connor's voice broke—damn, had he really been shouting?

Then—to Connor's surprise—Scott sat down on the sofa and started crying.

"Hell, Scott."

Connor found a box of tissues on the back of the toilet in the bathroom and brought it to his brother.

"I'm so sorry." Scott gasped. "I don't know how to be a brother."

"Why is it so hard for you? Why can't you just be nice?"

"Dad left. I know he was your dad and not mine, but he raised *me*. And then Mom was always going on about how talented you were, and then you turned out to be fucking queer, and it was always about you. 'No, Scott, we can't come to your game because Connor has a cold. No, Scott, we can't come to your award ceremony because Connor's art show is the same night.' And you have your fancy life now, and I have this house rotting around me and lawyer bills to pay for my divorce."

It was probably the most Scott had said to Connor in one stretch in over a decade, and it hit Connor like a ton of bricks.

"How," he gritted through his teeth, "is any of that *my* fault? You were eleven years older than me."

"And don't you think I feel like an asshole for being jealous of a baby all those years?"

"Jesus Christ, you're a piece of work." Connor glared at his brother. "You ever think about therapy?"

And just like that, Scott was laughing so hard, even more tears were falling. "Why do you think I'm such a fucking crybaby right now? I started seeing someone while Mandy and I were trying to work it out. Doc says my 'shields are thin,' whatever the fuck that means."

Connor shrugged. "Means exactly what it sounds like, I guess."

Scott wiped at his eyes. "I'm such a mess. I'm so angry, Con. I don't know why I'm always so angry, but this isn't how I saw my life, you know?"

Against his will, Connor felt a pang of empathy well up. Scott hadn't ever confided in Connor, but even Connor knew he hadn't planned to supervise a shift at a manufacturing plant for a living. There'd been football and scholarships and dreams. And then the wife and the house and an economy going to shit and divorce. But it wasn't an excuse.

"Maybe if you stop thinking the world owes you something, and start living your own life with some responsibility, you'd stop being so angry all the time."

Scott nodded. "My therapist says that. I'm sorry that you had to grow up with an asshole like me for a brother, but I'm what you've got."

It was probably half sarcasm, but Connor would take what he could get. "Apology accepted."

"I can't say that getting out of debt and finalizing my divorce is going to make me a decent person." Scott swallowed. "But Doc says I should rebuild bridges or some shit. I thought he meant with Mandy, but maybe he means everyone. So, if you want to get lunch or dinner after the closing, maybe we can start there."

A lump formed in Connor's throat. It was an olive branch, and an unexpected one after all these years. But he wasn't going to accept it at the expense of his self-respect.

"This is me rubbing your face in it." In spite of his harsh words, he made his voice as gentle as possible. "Scott, I'm always going to be gay. And I'm in love with Jed Jones. If you can't treat us with respect, I'm going to have to decline that invitation."

Scott wiped at his eyes again. "I have a lot to . . . to, what's that word my therapist uses—unpack? I'm an asshole, yeah. But I don't want to be alone forever, and you're the only family I've got. So I'll try to unpack my shit."

"Okay. Lunch or dinner after the closing. With me *and* my boyfriend. And if we can get through a meal together, civilly, we'll call that starting over."

He stood, and Scott followed. Connor held out his hand for a shake, and this time, Scott took it, giving his arm a solid pump before letting go. If he wiped his hand on his pants afterward, he at least waited until Connor had left.

Jed paced the front hallway, watching the snow come down fast and wet.

Where the hell was Connor? Jed shouldn't have let him go to Scott's alone. Connor had barely any experience driving in snow, and none recently. What the hell had they been thinking?

The afternoon sky was getting darker as the snow thickened, great big clumps forming before they even hit the ground. He didn't dare text, not wanting to distract Connor if he was behind the wheel.

He looked up Scott's number in the town directory and called, but Scott only said he'd left "ages ago."

He checked the weather reports, but they still said simply "Winter Weather Advisory" without the words "watch" or "warning" anywhere, so that was good right? Then where the fuck was Connor?

He called the state highway patrol, but they couldn't tell him about any accidents in the area, no matter how desperately he stuttered out the word please.

Was this what it meant to be in love? This spine-chilling, frantic terror that now that he'd finally found his happiness, it was being snatched away?

When he heard steps on the front porch, he ran to the door and flung it open.

"W-where the hell have you b-b-been?" he shouted at Connor, who shivered in his wool coat.

Connor gave him a blank stare, then pushed past him and into the house.

"Brrr. It's freezing out there. I was driving. It's snowing; it took longer."

"D-do you have any idea how w-w-worried I was?" Jed balled his hands into fists to keep from shaking Connor.

Connor just laughed. He fucking *laughed*. Just stood there, peeling out of his coat and hat, and laughed. "I'm fine, honey. I had to leave the car at the bottom of the hill though. Even four-wheel drive couldn't make that work."

"I am *not* fine," Jed ground through gritted teeth.

"Hey, I'm sorry. I should have texted. Come here." Connor held open his arms. "I'm not used to anyone caring whether I make it home on time for anything. I'll do better."

And just like that, he was holding Jed, and kissing him, and Jed's anger left him in a rush. Connor was fine, he was here, and Jed had his lips, and his hands, and his heart. When he came up for air, Jed held on to Connor. Closing his eyes, he said a silent prayer of thanks.

"Sc-scared me," he mumbled.

"I'm so sorry." Connor ran his hands up and down Jed's arms. "I love you."

"Love y-you, y-you jerk."

And then they were both laughing, and everything was okay.

"How'd it go with your family at brunch?" Connor asked.

"Surprisingly w-well. And Hannah's pr-pregnant, so that's bigger news. Took the h-heat off me." He searched Connor's eyes for some indication of how his own family meeting had gone. "Scott?"

Connor shook his head. "I don't know. He's still an asshole. But he's in therapy. Maybe wants to try to not be an asshole anymore."

"It's a st-start."

"Yeah. It is. I came this close—" Connor held up his fingers, a half inch apart, "—to decking him for scaring you Friday night."

"I'm g-glad you didn't." Jed kissed him. "Don't like the idea of my man in a fight."

Connor wrapped his arms around Jed's waist, and Jed delighted in being held. They were together, and this time, when Connor left, it would be to make his home *their* home.

"Come on, let's take a walk around the farm."

"It's sn-snowing."

"We can build a snowman!" Connor grinned. "Make snow angels too."

"W-we could go to bed and m-make out instead."

Connor nodded. "Yeah, we could. But I want to say good-bye to the old place. Can we do that?"

That's when it hit Jed that this was the last time Connor would see the farm. He didn't just want to play in the snow, but to make one final memory in this place that had been his home once.

"You g-got snow gear?"

Connor shook his head, and Jed went to the front closet. He pulled out the spare snowsuit.

"This is Mike's. It m-might fit you."

It didn't. The zipper strained, and the sleeves were too long, but Connor just shrugged, all good-natured, and pulled on a hat while Jed bundled up in his own snowsuit.

"You sh-sure you don't want to take the snowmo-mobile instead?"

"Can't have a snowball fight on the back of a snowmobile." Connor grinned and ran outside.

Jed followed, and got pelted with the first snowball just as he shut the door behind him. He scooped his own handful of snow off the porch and tossed. Missed. But it didn't matter. They were running and shouting and throwing snow, and he felt like a kid again.

Yeah, being in love was terrifying. But in its own way, it was fun too.

Epilogue

J ed's alarm went off just after midnight. The air conditioner in
the window wasn't running, and he was a little sticky with sweat,
but it wasn't too hot, despite being the middle of August. It was a
perfect night, and he intended to enjoy it. He reached across the bed
and found it empty.

That wasn't a surprise.

He'd learned that for all of Connor's early calls when he shot natural
light, he was actually a night owl, often working late. Sometimes, that
meant their schedules didn't mesh well. And sometimes, Connor's
work would take him away for a week or more at a time. Working
on someone else's farm meant Jed could take vacation time and go
with him—and they had. Jed had seen more of the world in the last
six months than he had in his whole life—but in the busiest summer
harvest time, that hadn't been possible, so they'd spent the past
week apart.

Jed stood and pulled on a pair of sweatpants, then padded out of
the bedroom. Connor sat at the table that divided the kitchen from
the rest of the apartment, laptop in front of him, with a little pair of
"they are *not* hipster glasses if you need them to see" perched on his
nose. His hair was messed up like he'd just run his hands through it.
Jed sat down next to Connor, who smiled up at him. He rolled his face
into Jed's shoulder and kissed his neck. It felt good, sexy and friendly
together—something else Jed was getting used to after a lifetime of
longing for it.

"Did I wake you up?" Connor asked. "I thought I kept the
music low."

Jed shook his head. "W-want to show you something."

Connor made a big show of lifting off his glasses to glance at Jed's lap.

"N-not that. C'mon." Jed grinned, stood again, and held out his hand. Connor closed the laptop and set his glasses down on top of it, then followed Jed out of the apartment to the common stairwell on the back side of the building.

"Where are we going?"

"The roof." Jed grinned, anticipation flooding him. He'd taken advantage of Connor's absence last week to get things ready, and he was lousy at keeping a secret. How many times had he been tempted to snap a photo with his phone and send it to Connor? He'd refrained only because the surprise on Connor's face would be worth it.

"Don't you spend enough time on rooftops during the day?" Connor teased.

"Not like this." Jed pushed open the roof access door, and Connor gasped.

No matter how much time Jed spent on rooftops, the views of New York took his breath away. He was still—definitely—a country boy, but he'd learned to appreciate the vast anonymous appeal of living in the city.

But the view wasn't what had drawn that gasp of surprise from Connor. Jed had brought the countryside here with him. In the small section of roof they'd designated as personal—not farm—space, a semicircle of dwarf top hat blueberry bushes in cheery terra-cotta containers offered up their late-summer fruit, and tomatoes on vines crawled up the trellis he'd leaned against the wall. A hammock for two stretched out invitingly between citronella torches. So it wasn't an air mattress in the back of an F-350; it was romantic in its own way.

When Jed climbed into it, Connor followed.

"This is nice." Connor snuggled into his shoulder. "I can't believe you did all this for me."

Jed pointed up at the sky. "It's Aug-gust fourteenth."

And Connor fell silent, watching the stars streak across the sky. The smile he turned on Jed was bright and unfettered, full of boyish enthusiasm. "I completely forgot."

"Another w-world," Jed reminded him. "But w-we can make it home any w-way we like."

"It's beautiful."

They watched in silence for a long time, a breeze off the river rocking the hammock ever so slightly.

"Remember how…" Connor gripped Jed through his sweatpants.

"Y-yeah." Jed's hand slid across the front of Connor's pants. "W was the most r romantic night."

They turned to each other in the hammock, hands raising goose bumps over skin even though they were both damp with sweat. They murmured soft words, loving words, and they kissed and touched with slow reverence until they came, first Connor, then Jed.

The meteor shower competed with the light of millions of lives in the sky over Brooklyn. But it didn't matter who won—they weren't living in two different worlds anymore.

With Connor in Jed's arms, they were both home.

Author's Note

Blandford, Massachusetts, is a charming hill town with roots going back before the American Revolution. As a young tween growing up there, I earned my summer cash picking blueberries on a farm very much like Jed's. New England in general, and rural New England in particular, are a curious mixture of puritanical roots and progressive ideals—exactly the kind of place that might produce men like Jed and like Connor.

For the architecture geeks, the "big white church" in Blandford is an early example of the colonial meetinghouse, and it's a historical landmark. The church no longer holds services, but it's far too pretty—and steeped in the community's history—to be left out of this story.

Dear Reader,

Thank you for reading Vanessa North's *Blueberry Boys*!

We know your time is precious and you have many, many entertainment options, so it means a lot that you've chosen to spend your time reading. We really hope you enjoyed it.

We'd be honored if you'd consider posting a review—good or bad—on sites like **Amazon, Barnes & Noble, Kobo, Goodreads, Twitter, Facebook, Tumblr,** and your blog or website. We'd also be honored if you told your friends and family about this book. Word of mouth is a book's lifeblood!

For more information on upcoming releases, author interviews, blog tours, contests, giveaways, and more, please sign up for our weekly, spam-free newsletter and visit us around the web:

Newsletter: tinyurl.com/RiptideSignup
Twitter: twitter.com/RiptideBooks
Facebook: facebook.com/RiptidePublishing
Goodreads: tinyurl.com/RiptideOnGoodreads
Tumblr: riptidepublishing.tumblr.com

Thank you so much for Reading the Rainbow!

RiptidePublishing.com

Acknowledgments

As always, I owe many thanks to many people—to Mishy Jo for her time and thoughtful explanations of the intersections of property and estate law. To Julio, Liz, and Liza for their thoughtful critique—and for believing in this story even when I was scared of it. To Sharis for those talks about faith and church. And of course to Caz, for making my words shine.

Y'all are the best.

Also by Vanessa North

Lake Lovelace Universe
Double Up
Rough Road

Two in Winter
Fight or Flight
Jackson's Law
Hostile Beauty
The Dark Collector
High and Tight
The Lonely Drop

The Ushers Trilogy
Amazon
United
Cracked

The Wiccan Haus
Shifter's Dance
Shifter's Song

Wild at Heart: Storm Haven
Under a Moonlit Night: Ripped Awake
Lucky's Charms: Seamus
Love in the Cards: Two of Wands

About the Author

Author of over a dozen novels, novellas, and short stories, Vanessa North delights in giving happy-ever-afters to characters who don't think they deserve them. Relentless curiosity led her to take up knitting and run a few marathons "just to see if she could." She started writing for the same reason. Her very patient husband pretends not to notice when her hobbies take over the house. Living and writing in Northwest Georgia, she finds her attempts to keep a quiet home are frequently thwarted by twin boy-children and a very, very large dog.

Website: vanessanorth.com
Twitter: twitter.com/vanessanwrites
Facebook: facebook.com/authorvanessanorth
Goodreads: goodreads.com/author/show/6436063.Vanessa_North

Enjoy more stories like *Blueberry Boys* at RiptidePublishing.com!

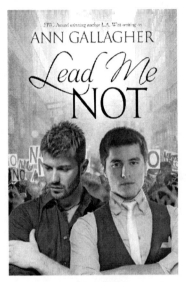

Lead Me Not
ISBN: 978-1-62649-278-3

Wedding Favors
ISBN: 978-1-62649-293-6

Earn Bonus Bucks!

Earn 1 Bonus Buck for each dollar you spend. Find out how at RiptidePublishing.com/news/bonus-bucks.

Win Free Ebooks for a Year!

Pre-order coming soon titles directly through our site and you'll receive one entry into a drawing for a chance to win free books for a year! Get the details at RiptidePublishing.com/contests.

CPSIA information can be obtained at www.ICGtesting.com
Printed in the USA
LVOW11s1737240316

480603LV00007B/602/P